MW00488514

THE WARRIOR
& THE WITCH

THE WARRIOR & THE WITCH

MEGAN MOON

Charleston, SC
www.PalmettoPublishing.com

The Warrior & The Witch

Copyright © 2021 by Megan Moon

All rights reserved

No portion of this book may be reproduced,
stored in a retrieval system, or transmitted in any form
by any means–electronic, mechanical, photocopy, recording,
or other–except for brief quotations in printed reviews,
without prior permission of the author.

First Edition

Hardcover ISBN: 978-1-63837-269-1
Paperback ISBN: 978-1-63837-257-8
eBook ISBN: 978-1-63837-665-1

Table of Contents

Prologue

Kepra walked into the tavern that was filled with thieves and smugglers. It reeked of zealous ego. Kepra visited this tavern specifically every time she visited Pi-Ramesses; it reminded her so much of how she began her journey and found herself. This tavern was where she and Ankh had their first discussion of the real reason she was in the palace. The great city that her parents had built was now called Qantir, but it still held a special place in her heart. Kepra walked into the tavern. Everyone stopped and looked in the beautiful warrior's direction. Immediately, she was looked upon as meat; no one dared think someone so beautiful could be so dangerous. Someone out of the crowd yelled, "that's Kepra, the warrior goddess!".

The crowd gasped and started heading out of the tavern in fear that she was there to take one of them in for a crime they had committed. Kepra was the undefeated warrior of her time, and everyone from Rome to Egypt had her name on their lips. Kepra peered through the anxious group that was hastily trying to vacate the tavern when she saw a hooded character sitting down at a table. As she approached the chair across from the mysterious character, she asked, "is this seat taken?" The hooded figure pulled the hood slightly off their face, only revealing enough for Kepra to recognize them. It was her old friend Ankh.

"Please sit, goddess," he said. Kepra was elated to see him; it had been way too long. Ankh hid his face again for fear of someone noticing him. Before Kepra could sit down, he got up and greeted her with a hug. He and Kepra sat down and got right down to business. Ankh had sent for Kepra; he had had unexplainable dreams. He was scared that they might come true and asked Kepra to do some recon. Kepra agreed to the assignment. Ankh could not help himself to bring up the past. Seeing her brought back all kinds of memories for him.

Ankh said, "Kepra, before you leave"—he grabbed her hand while he was talking—"do you remember this tavern?".

She smiled and sat back down. "I do. I remember it like it was yesterday, how could I forget," she said as she looked around the old tavern. He asked her to refresh his memory, as they had never talked about everything that exactly happened. The day she left was the saddest day of his life. He wanted to hear Kepra's whole story. "Ankh, I must get to the task you have given me. Your life might be at risk," she informed him.

"It can wait a little while longer, Kepra. I am safe when I am with you," he said. So, they requested more ale from the bartender, and she began her story of what was...

Chapter 1
A New Addition

A long time ago, when the sunsets danced on the peeks of the pyramids of Giza, and the pharaohs looked to Orion's belt for help from the gods, there was a queen and king. Ramesses the ii and Nefertari were the pharaohs of Egypt. The pharaohs were known for being devoted servants to the gods. In everything they did, they would first consult with them and seek their guidance. The king and queen also made sure always to do what was best for their people, and the gods admired that about them. They were selfless. In return, the gods made sure they were rewarded for their love and devotion. Their lands always possessed bountiful harvests; the cattle were always healthy, and trade was at an all-time peak. Their land was always fortuitous. The queen and king were well-loved by everyone in the Egyptian empire because they knew without the pharaohs 'loyalty to the gods, their lands would not be so fortunate. The gods watched over them for years and saw that Nefertari was trying to conceive. With so much faith given to the gods from the queen and king, the gods decided to bless them with a gift they would surely cherish forever. On the second night of the winter solstice, the gods bestowed upon the queen and king a beautiful baby girl. The pharaohs were so pleased with the little bundle of joy. In tribute to the gods, they decided to name her after one of the gods. The pharaohs called her "Kepra" after the god Kepra, who represents the rising sun. It was the brightest thing that ever happened in the pharaohs 'lives.

It had been just over a year after the queen had given birth, and Egypt was at war with the Hittites. It was the battle of Kadesh. The once-beautiful place they had called home, which had thrived with life and had looked so ethereal, was now desecrated and being destroyed. It was chaos throughout the streets of the city of Thebes. The Hittites weren't leaving hardly anything or anyone standing, including women and children. The pharaoh sounded the alarm, and the Egyptians stood their ground and decided to drive them out of the city. It was one of the biggest chariot wars of all time, Egypt's ten thousand men to the Hittites 'massive fifty thousand men; Hittites knew that they were at a huge advantage. The kingdom was falling into ruins, leaving nothing but rubble. The mighty divisions that rode with Ramesses the ii dispersed into four sectors, which left the city very vulnerable. Two of the sectors went to the city; the other two split up. The Hittites ended up surprising one group of the great pharaoh's men and demolished one of his four divisions. The Hittites continued forward to pillage and loot the city of Thebes. Pharaoh made it to the city of Kadesh and had it surrounded. With so many of the Hittites 'men. Gone, there was no one there to protect it. He noticed that the other divisions had not made it to the city, so the king turned his chariots around and headed back toward Thebes.

He was nervous about the small numbers of soldiers left in Kadesh as if it were a trap. "Where have they all gone?" He thought. As fast as the horses could carry them, they rushed back to the city. They crossed the Nile, and the king saw that his city was in distress. He thought about his wife and child and then whispered, "my family." He took off fighting and striking the Hittites. Seeing the magnitude of the Hittites had the pharaoh thinking things were hopeless, but he didn't give up. He kept swinging his sword, trying to get back to his family. The fight lasted for hours. The sun finally vanished, and the chief of commanders came to Ramesses and told him to retreat and regroup until the morning light. It took the commander and most of his men to tear Ramesses away from the fight. All he could do was hope they did not find his wife and child. He prayed and kept hope that the protection he'd put in place for them did not fail. Ramesses and his army retreated outside the city, close enough to see what the Hittites were doing to figure out a plan of attack. The Hittites believed the battle was already won. Nefertari was worried that the Hittites breached the palace gates and were inside destroying everything. The Hittites celebrated their victory in the city, and everyone was either drunk or taking Thebes village women to their beds.

Before the Hittites entered the palace gates, Nefertari noticed they were getting closer and witnessed her soldiers falling one by one. She decided to dress herself and her baby in all black. She wore a satin scarf over her face and head and a hood that kept her discreet. She decided she had to leave the palace. They were getting too close, so just before the Hittites broke into the palace, she remembered a secret passage that her husband told her about just in case she needed safety and he was not there to protect her. She went to their bedroom and looked around, trying to remember where the lever was for the secret passage. She closed her eyes and then looked right at a candle holder on the wall next to a sculpture. She walked over and pulled the latch disguised as a candle holder. It unlocked a door in the floor, and it opened! She took Kepra and walked down the stairs of the secret room. There was a lever on the inside that sealed the door shut. She pulled it, and the door automatically closed. There were cobwebs and dust all over the place. She could hardly see; all she could feel were the rocks and dirt under her feet.

She looked to the torches that seemed not to have been lit in years. She placed Kepra on the ground and reached for two rocks. She quickly hit them over one of the torches, and it lit. She took the first torch in one hand and Kepra in the other and started walking down a path. She lit every torch as she went by them. Eventually, Nefertari reached a room. The room was small but just enough to sit in and wait with her baby. Before she went into the room, she noticed the path still went on; she decided to see where it led. She went farther and farther, finally getting to a wall that seemed like it opened. She searched with the torch, trying to figure out the mystery of the wall. She finally looked up and saw a lever. Nefertari pulled on the lever, careful not to drop or disturb her sleeping daughter. The wall quickly went up. The wall was behind trees and plants unseen by the naked eye. She made sure her hood was on her head and her scarf fit tightly around her face as she went out into the night.

During all of this, Nefertari's faith was not changed. She continued to pray and pray, but it seemed like the gods were nowhere to be found. It was as if they were not listening to her. The queen, who had lost all hope at this point, was devastated and felt alone for the first time. She was hearing her people scream and die throughout the city. She was beginning to think that the war was over. Her city had succumbed to the Hittites 'commands. The queen thought of any sources that would heal her country from the disastrous war and bring her loving husband back to her safely.

The queen started to think as she walked and decided that if anyone could protect her daughter and her country, it would be Neith, the goddess of war. Avoiding all the guards and carefully sneaking through the dark streets and cold alleyways, the queen finally reached the middle of the city that held the fascinating bronze-and-ochre temple of the goddess Neith. She was relieved that the temple had remained intact. The queen looked around before entering the temple, and after seeing the coast was clear, she headed in. When she entered, a golden statue looked as high as a pyramid, with a beautiful woman with a crown worn only by the pharaohs. The golden statue was surrounded by beautiful gifts, offerings with candles, and lit incense. The smell of kapet surrounded the temple. The queen slowly approached the statue with her baby in her arms. She soon after knelt before the statue and started praying. The queen placed the baby before the statue and left Kepra there. With tears in her eyes, the queen knew the gods would only listen if she gave them a gift they could not refuse. With so much turmoil in her mind and heart, she continued to pray while hearing her city fall outside the temple.

The pharaoh could wait no longer. He decided to take back the city with the remaining soldiers. There was no more time for them to rest. The pharaoh wanted to attack. The king had seen the men getting drunk and celebrating their so-called victory earlier. While the men slept, the pharaoh thought it would be best for them to take the given opportunity. The pharaoh gathered the remaining soldiers and quietly sneaked into the kingdom to assassinate the rest of the Hittites. As the Egyptians were killing the soldiers, some of them began to wake up and attack. The king and the Egyptians fought like it was the last battle they would ever see when suddenly, one of the divisions that separated from the pharaoh's army showed up. The king was more than grateful that his men had arrived. When the infantry came, they demolished all of the Hittites. The Hittites retreated and ran across the Nile. The Egyptians had momentarily won the war.

When the king was done fighting, he and the soldiers stormed the palace, searching for his wife and child. He was nervous. His heart felt like it was in his stomach, and he felt every beat. He searched every room; there was no sign of her. He then remembered the secret room and opened it. He saw the torches lit and ran along the path to the room. There she was fast asleep. He woke her up and hugged her; she was thrilled. He kissed her and asked her if she was all right. She nodded. He looked around in search of the baby and could not find her. "Nefertari, where is Kepra?".

She thought for a moment and then started to put her hands on her face and began to cry hysterically. He said, "what is it? Where is she, Nefertari? Tell me.".

She couldn't say a word. He picked her up and headed in the direction of the palace. He placed her on the bed. She was mute and just kept staring in front of her like her body had lost its soul. The pharaoh ran to his guards and said, "search the entire kingdom for Kepra. Tear it down if you have to; I need to find my baby." He ran back to console the queen.

She told him she didn't know how she even got back into the palace. All she could remember was going to the temple of Neith. He looked at her confused. "There was so much going on last night. You could have been killed. What was so important you had to go to the temple?" He asked.

She shook her head and lied to the king. "I went to pray for our city, Ramesses; it felt as if the gods did not hear my prayers, so I went to them," she said. She told him that was the last place that she remembered seeing the baby. With despair written over both of their faces and tears in the king's eyes, he got up from the queen, and he ran to the temple of Neith. With hope still running through his veins, he entered the temple in disbelief that his daughter was gone. He searched high and low in the extremely high vaulted temple of the goddess, destroying all of the sacrifices and offerings. He begged and begged the gods and goddess to bring back their daughter. Cursing them and dropping to his knees, he cried out, "we have been nothing but good to you. Why would you take her from us? Where is she?" He pleaded again with them. "Where is she?" He sobbed in the temple. There was nothing more he could do; she was gone. He rose from his knees and headed to the soldiers again.

"Someone has taken the princess. Continue looking for her; we will not give up. We do not need the gods." He stormed off to seek out his wife. When he got to her, he asked if she remembered anything else about the night. "She was not there, Nefertari. I searched the entire temple. She's gone," he said with tears running down his face.

She thought to herself for a moment before answering him. She honestly did not know why they had won the war, so she assumed that the gods heard her prayer and took the offering she left. She knew not, though, the worst part of it all, being left in the confusion of what happened. She knew she could not tell her husband of the horrific thing she tried to do to please the gods. She could not look into his eyes and tell him why she thought they won the battle. She knew it was her offering their baby girl up to the gods, if she was really gone. Nefertari didn't have the courage or the heart to break his. She looked at him and said, "I do not remember the night, husband." He told her he had every guard looking for her in the city. He was hopeful the queen saw that. She agreed that it was a good idea. She was hopeful as well.

Months passed, and the couple was still in search of their child. They offered rewards and even looked beyond the city of Thebes. They grew tired of the city. The heart-wrenching feeling came to them every time they would pass her room, so they decided to move to a new city and create a new capital. They did not want to remember the loss of their child. Ramesses was tired of his wife's nightmares and sleepwalking. He wanted to heal. They needed to heal. Ramesses thought of an idea to go forward and start some new memories. The king took on an empire at this point. His kingdom was called the new kingdom, and it ran along the Nile River up into Kadesh. Ramesses learned to avoid anything like that happening again, so he made peace treaties among the cities for him to do so. So, Egypt grew and grew. Ramesses and his wife moved to Pi-Ramesses, a city whose name meant "the house of Ramesses." In just a few years, the city of Pi-Ramesses was thriving with life, and the couple was expecting a new baby.

Chapter 2

Aaru

The night the queen came to see Neith, the streets were drowned in the Egyptians 'red blood. The smell of crimson was throughout the city, and it was a bloodbath. Neith was aware that Nefertari was approaching the temple. There wasn't a moment that she could go without hearing the cries coming from the queen and the city of Thebes. Everyone seemed to be praying, so Neith proceeded to her temple to wait for the queen without hesitation. When the queen got to the temple, Neith immediately saw her, but she waited in the shadows to avoid bringing attention to herself. She did not desire the queen to know she was there. Neith saw Nefertari walk over to the large statue of her, and she saw the queen's many attempts of trying to put the baby down as an offering with streams of water flowing from her face. Neith was pleased. Despite the queen's heart breaking, she still had enough faith to give her one irreplaceable thing. Still in the darkness, the goddess continued to watch the queen's every move, but Neith grew impatient waiting for the woman to leave. Neith thought of a plan that would make the queen tired and put her into a deep sleep. The aroma in the room switched its smell to that of lavender little by little. It began to take over the entire temple. There was smoke everywhere. The queen could barely keep her eyes open when she passed out next to the baby. Neith acted quickly, remembering the chaos that was happening outside.

She grabbed the baby and the queen and transported the three to the kingdom in the secret room Nefertari had found just before going to the temple . This room made sure to keep the royal family safe in case of invasion from outsiders or opposing armies. She left the queen on the chair sleeping and then vanished into thin air. Neith took Kepra, and they disappeared together.

The next day Neith came to see whether the vile creatures who had raided the kingdom still left her temple unharmed. When she advanced toward the temple, everything on the outside seemed normal. She knew with the battle being won, the people would rejoice that the gods were on their side once again, but to her disbelief, she saw only statues and offerings broken and badly defiled when she entered the temple. Gold had been taken; her statues 'heads were on the floor, no longer attached to the bodies. Some of the bodies were cracked; some were shattered into pieces. The temple doors had been left open with no priest to watch, which led to animals coming inside and feasting on her food. Neith began to get angry after gifting the Egyptians with a victory that would not have been won without her help. "Insignificant humans!" She yelled as she kicked a pottery bowl across the room. She began to feel the rage inside her and immediately vowed vengeance against the pharaohs and humanity. She would never allow the queen and king the opportunity to see their child again, and their people will have bad harvests and sick cattle for many moons as long as they stayed in Thebes.

Neith and Kepra continued going back and forth from the underworld and Aaru. Kepra grew up her whole life only knowing Neith as her mother that she had spat her out, and she became what she was: a living, breathing goddess. With Neith, the goddess of war, being her mom, she was given the title "young goddess of war." Orion's belt was where majority of all the gods lived; it was beautiful. Another name for it was

Aaru. It was usually placed in the east, where the sun rises. It possessed lush green boundless reed fields like those of the earthly Nile. Plants and animals of each kind surrounded it. It had countless hunting and farming for the souls to live peacefully for eternity. It was ethereal with multiple islands; right in the middle of the islands was a palace where the gods resided. The palace was vaulted so high that the clouds would play hide-and-seek with the peak of its columns. It was adorned in beautiful whites and golds, with vines growing inside and out. It was an angelic place.

While they were in the heavens, Neith trained Kepra in the courtyards of the palace every day. She wanted Kepra to be the strongest warrior of all the gods. Day by day, she got stronger; she couldn't wait until the day she would be strong enough to take on the best in all the cosmos, her mother and Horus, the god of war. Neith gave her every combat move she knew, from melee to swords and even archery. She was a jack of all trades. As Kepra began to get older, she started training on her own, sometimes for hours at end. Most nights would disappear into the morning, and she would be bruised from trying to invent her tactics. Kepra practiced so much that Neith would have to make the young warrior come in and rest. Kepra grew, and as she grew, so did her strength at rapid speed. She was beginning to see all she had worked for coming to fruition, and she was proud of herself. One of the famous moves that she was working on was striking without seeing. She would blindfold herself and then have four wooden stumps around her. Every time nut the sky goddess would make the wind turn, Kepra would place her attention on the wood and hit it, depending on what direction she would hear. Eventually, she had to branch out and find someone to help her with this move. Kepra felt she had hit a plateau when it came to training, so she sought out the god of war.

Kepra had begun to train with Horus; he elevated her strength and stamina far past her expectations. She showed him the technique that she tried before but wasn't working because the precision of the wind. She needed someone to come at her while she was blindfolded so she could hear how a fist sounded, aiming in her direction. So, they plunged into the method. He taught her how to deal with more than five foes. The tactic she had learned without seeing had developed. Horus would dance around her quietly, with Kepra being blindfolded. He would throw daggers for her to catch; he would put a sword in her hand and ask her to block and attack, or even catch with her bare hands. The technique that she had brought to Horus had gotten so advanced that she was shooting and catching arrows after they were done with the blindfold still attached. He was impressed. He taught her many more extremely skilled techniques she wouldn't have excelled in if not for him. Seeing each other every day, the two grew to become the greatest of friends, and their bond started just like a droplet of water to a newly planted seed. Kepra was determined to make Neith proud of her. Because her mom was the goddess of war, she felt more pressure in learning all there was to learn about war and strategy. She continued striving to train. She became obsessed with infinite strength and being a perfectionist.

Kepra, being the persistent warrior that she was, wanted to learn all the fundamentals in war and know everything there was about being a great warrior. She not only trained in brute strength, but she also trained her mind. For she knew her mind was a dangerous thing when activated. She knew that her strength came from her inner self as much as it was physical. She wanted to know how to tap into her spirit if she could not use a weapon. She wanted to know the ins and outs of every battle that was won and lost, and if they lost, why they did. She trained her mind to develop a counterattack for every attack, and vice versa. She was beginning to become dangerous.

She knew that to get to the mental freedom that she so desired, she needed the help of Thoth, the most intelligent god. Thoth admired and enjoyed seeing Kepra's lust to learn. He saw that she was intrigued with knowledge as much as he, and because of that made her a better warrior than he had ever seen. Thoth was the god of wisdom, writing, science, magic, and more, but Thoth's true gift was the amount of wisdom he possessed. He was among the few that were the original gods. Kepra would ask Thoth about their history. She was interested in all the gods; there were so many that she could not keep up. Thoth, being the good teacher that he was, taught her about them; he started as far back as the beginning of time. He explained to her why some gods were like others and why some took on the names of others. To Kepra its was all very confusing, but she still tried to keep up and understand. Kepra looked into not just their history but also everyone else's religions. She studied martial arts techniques and practiced them in her own time. She studied the pressure points in the body and how to paralyze a person in one strike. She studied the Greeks 'and Viking's combats and their war techniques. She learned a lot by being with Thoth, and like Horus, Kepra and Thoth became close fast.

Kepra's friendships with the two gods escalated quickly. There were arguments and fights between the two men constantly over winning the beautiful goddess's love. She began to find herself in a love triangle. The hard thing for Kepra was that she adored both of them. There was always a doe-eyed look on her face when either one of them was nearby. They were both so different, yet their love for her was the same. The two gods did not enjoy having to share her. They hated that Kepra could not choose between the two. Her birthday was approaching, and the time to outshine and show her who loved her the most was on both of the gods top priority.

Kepra's birthday finally arrived, and it was not just any birthday; it was her eighteenth birthday. She expected to be treated like a woman instead of a child. She wanted nothing more than to travel the cosmos. She had been stuck at the palace her whole life. She felt it was finally time to spread her wings and venture out. There was a great celebration in the heavens that day for the newly admired young goddess of war. The party was accented in beautiful shades of green, which was her favorite color; it was also draped with satin golds, whites, and ivory. There were beautiful exotic birds with millions of different colors, and there were unique-looking horses, some with wings, some with horns, and some with both. The horses consisted of all different colors: black, white, brown, and multicolor. Every majestic beast that the gods created was in attendance, as was every god of importance. The party had sheers cascading around the outside where the party was, and Amun-ra made sure to make the sunshine as bright as the warrior of wars smile. When she arrived from the palace she was already blindfolded, Neith walked her down the palace stairs and revealed the festivities. Everyone was dancing and drinking; there was live music played by an orchestra that quickly switched songs to show that the goddess had finally arrived. Everyone looked so happy to see her, and once everyone acknowledged she was there, they sang a song in celebration of her. She had grown into a beautiful woman with curly darkish-brown hair accented with hints of the sun, that descended to the middle of her back. Her skin was as smooth and popped with melanin, the same color brown as the sand in the deserts of Egypt. She was of average height with a body that made Hathor, the goddess of love, jealous.

For her birthday, she was given an alarming number of gifts. Some of those gifts consisted of her armor; the great god

Ptah himself had made it. Ptah was the god of craftsmen, pottery, and creation. The armor was dark leather accented with pure gold. The armor came in two pieces. There was a skirt cut in two sectors on each hip, with a crisscross in the middle of the skirt. The armor came with bracers and a scarab beetle in the middle of the breast plate made of moonstone. It was also accented with gold wings in the middle surrounding the scarab beetle's body. The top was form-fitting and caressed her body just enough to show off Kepra's curves.

Kepra was also given a sword from the great Amun-ra. It was called the light in darkness. It was one of the most powerful swords in the world. Amun-ra was one of the creators of the universe. He'd not seen little Kepra since she was nothing but a baby, but even as a child, he would notice she would train her heart away. He saw her build up so much inner and outer strength. He had never seen a goddess work as hard as Kepra did. Amun had grown fond of the little girl and knew that it was surely her if anyone deserved this sword. The sword presented to Kepra was like none other and possessed extraordinary power to whoever knew how to wield it correctly. He looked at her and said, "you may not be able to unlock its power now, but the time will come when you will understand it, and it will understand you, young one.".

That day was full of laughs and fun for Kepra, along with a lot of flirting coming from the two gods who had been training her over the years. Horus was an attractive man. He wore gold-and-bronze armor with the emblem of a falcon in the middle of his breastplate. He was muscular and fit with skin the color of the night sky. He had a beard that was perfectly tapered and aligned with a mustache on top of his luscious lips. His hair was short, black, curly, and kinky. His hair was faded on each side and thick in the middle, showing his hair's style as a mohawk. His muscles peeked out from the armor he wore, and his legs looked chiseled from a statue. He looked radiant in his seductive aura. Even though Thoth was considered more brain than brawn, he was still very fit. He wore a white-and-gold shendyt with his chest out. He also wore a headdress that had an ibis on the top of it. His skin was slightly darker than Kepra's complexion, and he had short black hair that looked like the sea formed pools of waves on it. He was taller than Horus and his eyes twinkled with every beautifully white smile he gave. Horus and Thoth had grown an emotional attachment to the new goddess, and Kepra was blind to it all the same. She had a feeling that the two gods enjoyed her company but never to the degree that they wanted. Kepra had devoted all of her time and energy to being the perfect warrior. The thought of love never crossed her mind. The two gods would have to work hard to make Kepra see that they were fighting for her love.

Kepra sneaked away from the ceremony, pulling back the sheers and vines, walking toward the edge of the palace to the railing. She peered into the heavens to look upon earth, not realizing the connection she felt to the half-sea-half-land planet, with no knowledge of her birth family residing there. Kepra didn't notice, but someone was walking behind her and observing a different view. Horus had gotten closer to check on her. Horus tried to call out to Kepra, but her fascination was still placed on the planet. When she finally came to, she noticed Horus next to her. She apologized for not being completely aware of his presence. He asked her if she was ok, and she admitted she was: "I just needed a breather. It was getting a little overwhelming for me in there." They talked for a little bit about how she was enjoying the party and the events of the day. He then began to see her focus shift again to the planet. He was intrigued at this point and asked Kepra what the significance of the planet meant to her. She paused and then looked over at him and said, "I honestly don't know. It is not like it's more beautiful than any other one that I've seen rotating through the heavens on an everyday basis. I can't explain it, but there is something about it.".

He told her that they visit that particular globe, that they were worshipped throughout all of Egypt, a continent that resided on the earth. Earth was the name of the planet. She looked at him and said, "I know; Thoth taught me all about the planet and how they gift the gods with all sorts of things so that the gods will be in their favor.".

He looked at her with jealousy in his eyes. "So, you and Thoth talk a lot about the gods, I see," he said.

"Thoth is my teacher just like you, and just like you, both of you have a special place in my heart. Without either of you, I wouldn't be who I am. I am very appreciative of you both," she said.

He stopped and looked away from her; he stared off into the distance for a while and then said, "Kepra, what if we both want to be with you? Did you even know we both have the desire to be yours?".

She said, "no, I had no clue, and where is all this coming from, Horus? Why haven't you two told me? It is my birthday; I don't want to talk about this now.".

He shook his head. "Everyone in our realm knows, Kepra. Fine; I won't say anything else about it," he said. There was an awkward pause. He thought at that moment that he should just shut up, but instead, he looked at Kepra and said, "I'm sorry. I get overly jealous when you talk about him." He took her chin in his hand and looked into her brown eyes. "I want to be the only one, and I need you to know that.".

He pulled her face closer, and they kissed passionately. It was like nothing Kepra had ever felt. She was dazed and completely helpless to his touch. His lips felt like velvet on hers, and she could feel the love that he possessed for her transferring from his body onto her lips. When he finally moved away, he said, "how was that?".

She blushed and shook her head. "It was nice.".

They both smiled, and he licked his lips. He said, "that wasn't your surprise, though. I do have the great warrior of war a gift." Horus, who had set a big chest on the ground behind her before engaging in conversation with her, looked back and walked over to the chest. He picked it up and brought it closer to her. He asked her to open the chest. She could hear sounds coming from inside. She was excited. When she finally opened the chest, she saw a baby male lion cub in it. He was purring and looking up at her as if saying, "take me.".

He had golden hazel eyes and a yellowish-brown tint to his soft coat. He had little spurts of hair around his head where his mane would be, and he was already half the size of her. Horus.

Told her that he would get as big as a horse, "big enough for you to ride and faster than any animal. He will be protective and intelligent. Whenever you call, he will listen." Kepra's eyes lit up, and she was so excited she pulled closer to Horus. They were about to solidify Kepra's second kiss.

When all of a sudden Neith came through the satin sheers and interrupted the two, asking Kepra to return to the party. "Everyone is looking for you, Kepra. What has been keeping you so long?" Neith said. Kepra, with cub in hand, apologized to her mother and began walking shoulder to shoulder with Horus. As they walked, they began to laugh among themselves and reentered the party. She whispered to him, "thank you. It is an amazing gift, Horus." Kepra looking at the baby cub and decided to call him Aten.

Horus and Kepra, while entering the party, saw everyone socializing and celebrating. There was a toast to the goddess. Thoth, the god of wisdom, who adored the warrior, decided to chime in and give a toast. He said, "to the beautiful woman that is going to give the cosmos a hell of a time conquering anything that gets in her way of honor and success. I present this gift to you." As he bowed, six of the workers that live among the gods to keep the palace looking as magnificent as it did came around Thoth with a box dripped in bronze. It had a sphinx head on the lock. She walked over slowly to the trunk with very intricate designs surrounding the lock and then bent down to see what was in it. When Kepra opened the box, it was a glow that peered from within, letting out just enough for Kepra to see. It was a papyrus that looked like it was made of gold with red lettering. When she unraveled the paper, it read, "to Kepra: one trip to any planet to see any species of your choosing, accompanied by Thoth on your mother's approval only.".

She was overwhelmed with joy and immediately hugged Thoth. Horus rolled his eyes and crushed the glass that was in his hand. The gods in the background who played instruments and dancing had continued, and Thoth asked the beautiful goddess for her hand in a dance. Kepra blushed and nodded. Thoth took her hand, and they started dancing. The dance seemed so unreal. She was so close to Thoth; she could smell him. He smelled like the rain forest with wildflowers and berries.

The two danced for a while. Eventually, Horus's ego wouldn't allow it any longer. With both of the gods knowing they both an emotional connection with Kepra, they would sometimes fight for her affection, but tonight it got to the point of hatred. Horus came over and asked for the goddess's hand to dance, and Thoth looked at his hand and danced away with Kepra. Horus, embarrassed and ego bruised, approached Thoth and Kepra one last time. "Thoth, allow me a dance with the woman of the hour, please," Horus said.

Thoth smirked and said, "don't you know it's rude, god of war, to try to budge yourself into our dance as if it is some battle? We are dancing together. Catch her later if she has time for you.".

Kepra, looking at Horus getting upset, chimed in and said, "guys, it's ok. I can dance with Horus; now it's not that serious. Thoth, we have danced for a while; it is time." Thoth, pissed at Horus, shook his hand and said, "my apologies, god of war," and then pulled him closer for a hug. While Thoth was hugging the god, he whispered in his ear, "she doesn't want you, Horus; just accept it.".

Horus this time balled up his hand and punched Thoth away from her, and they start to fight to the point that Amun had to get in the middle and break it up, but they continued. The crowd dispersed and decided to watch the travesty that was happening. Kepra, who was on the sidelines, stepped in before one of them could draw a weapon or summon a spell. She blocked both of them. She looked at them with disappointment. How can two people that claimed to care for her show so much disrespect on her birthday? How could they disrupt such a magical day? She stared at them, her eyes with rage in them going back and forth from Thoth and Horus. She looked at them and shouted, "I am not an item or a war you can win with good gestures and gifts, nor am I a mere whore that you can speak sweet nothings to, and I take your bedside. You two will leave me alone for the remainder of the night. I wish nothing to do with either of you. Good night, everyone." She picked Aten up and ran into the palace.

Neith announced to the crowd that at the party, "thank you for coming, and thank you for the grand gifts that you have given to Kepra, but as of right now, the party is over." While everyone was leaving, Neith slowly became more and more upset that her daughter's party was destroyed and that her daughter had to leave in such a distressed manner. As Neith past the gods Horus and Thoth, she looked at them from head to toe and then straight at the castle and said, "you two are among the oldest gods. You would think you could contain yourself over an eighteen-year-old girl." As she left them, she said, "good night, gentlemen.".

They looked at each other and shook their heads. They knew they had messed up their chances with Kepra if any at all were there before. They disappeared soon after.

After the party and everyone returned to normal, Kepra looked out to see when everyone had completely left the courtyard. Kepra decided to go back out into the courtyard to get her mind off of the unfortunate events and started showing Aten how to fight. Kepra thought to herself she would train him to be her backup. If things ever got out of hand, he would be very useful. She showed him how to walk without being detected. She taught him how to channel his inner strength and project it outward. He had grown stronger over the coursing days, and he grew bigger with each training session. At this point, Aten was bigger than any horse she had ever seen. When Kepra noticed that Aten wasn't going to get any bigger, she decided to hop on his back for the first time and give him a ride around the heavens. Aten dropped down so that the goddess could get on his back, and she put one foot over him, and he got up with a jolt and took off running in the wind. Flying around the palace felt amazing and exhilarating. Whenever the gods had to get around, it was more like teleportation than flying. It happened so quickly that you missed out on all the beauty the cosmos had to offer. They rode around for hours, getting him used to her weight. He had to be able to do everything Kepra had taught him, but now with her on him. So, after their flight, they came down back to the palace and repeated everything that he knew how to do, just this time with her on him. He quickly learned and picked up with valiant interest to become all that Kepra wanted him to be she loved Aten. Outside of Thoth and Horus, he was the first living thing that she considered a real friend.

One evening during one of the sessions Kepra was having with Aten, Horus had stopped by to check on the magnificent feline and asked Kepra how everything was coming along with the beast. She looked at him and smiled, thanking him once again for giving him to her. She told him she didn't know what she did before she had him. Flirtatiously, Kepra asked, "as you can see, though, god of war, we are training. Can I help you with anything?" They laughed and talked some more. Kepra was done for the night training Aten and told him to eat, and she would see him later. He walked over, nuzzled her leg as she petted him; then he disappeared into the night.

Horus had been waiting for a moment alone with Kepra for a long time. It had been months after the confrontation with Thoth at her party. He could still tell she was upset with him.

He had felt the pain to well with her silence, for every time they would be around each other, she would act as if he was nothing more than air. Tonight, would be different.

Tonight, would be the night he would ask her for his forgiveness and profess his love for her. Horus and Kepra walked to a part of Orion's belt that was parted just enough to see the stars shinning and certain planets aligning. The two were so connected with each other's energy that they didn't even notice that someone was there the entire time, watching their every movement. The two were captivated by each other. It was a magical experience, and the two, engulfed in each other, floated to a nearby cloud. Horus pressed Kepra's back on the cloud, and the two immediately began to invade each other's bodies. After the romantic relations they had, he looked at her body in all its wonders and apologized for making a spectacle of himself at her party and told her he loved—.

Before he could utter another word, she took her finger, placed it on his mouth, and silenced him. "Do not say what you are about to say, god of war; just show me," she said, and they continued to become one with each other's souls once again.

22

The next day Neith, Kepra's mother, asked her to visit the underworld and see Anubis. Kepra excitedly hugged her mom and agreed to go. Kepra was only a child when they visited the underworld last. Neith thought that it would do her some good to get her out of the palace. Anubis was the god of the afterlife who guided lost souls and dealt with mummification. Neith gave her special tasks. While in the underworld, she asked her daughter to ask Anubis about the death of two humans. She walked over to Kepra and put her cheek in her hand. While looking in her eyes, Neith said, "you mustn't forget to ask him, Kepra, all right?" Neith failed to mention who they were, but Kepra cared less and sought after the god of the dead.

Right before she set off, Neith stopped Kepra and said, "oh, and Kepra, also ask him if there is anything that would prevent it? He will know what I mean.".

Kepra asked her mother, "what do these humans have to do with us, and why do I have to ask him?".

Neith looked at her and said, "do as I say, please.".

She agreed, but Kepra was still confused about why she had to be involved with mortal life and that her mother for that matter even cared for them. Kepra got on the back of Aten, and they descended to the underworld to seek out the god Anubis. Kepra had been to the underworld before, but never as a mature adult. She felt liberated and nervous all at the same time. She was wary of the place because of all the deadly things she heard that existed there. The gods who did not live among them in the palace lived in the underworld with the demons. Kepra, with adrenaline in her veins, thought out loud to herself, "I know that we can defeat any obstacle that will be put in our way; isn't that right, Aten?" Aten roared in agreement to assure Kepra, but Kepra had no idea what lay ahead in the mysterious, dark Duat.

Chapter 3
A Gift in The Duat

K epra and Aten had finally got to the gates of the underworld. It was a dreary place filled with fire and magma. The roads were burned, and lamps hung from the wall that lit up the way for the souls to see. The roads were exalted from the ground itself. They had just enough room to walk one by one due to the statues. The statues on each side consisted of three gods: Anubis, Horus, and Osiris. They were massive in size and the color of gold. The place smelled horrific. It smelled of flesh burning mixed with wax. The souls would start their journey where the statues began. The souls would descend into the underworld, and then they would meet with the god Osiris. It was the first familiar face that Kepra noticed on arrival while riding Aten.

She stopped on the path and said hello to Osiris. He greeted her with a hug and asked her what the special occasion was. She told him how her mother wanted her to see Anubis and familiarize herself with the underworld. She asked Osiris if he knew the quickest way to get to him. He looked at her while scratching the back of his head with a wince on his face. "He would more than likely be at the front of the line of souls. It would take you some time to get there.".

She pointed to Aten and said, "he flies.".

He then looked over his shoulder and pointed in the direction she should head. She got back on Aten and thanked him, waved, and then the two ascended in the air. He called out to her while she was in the air: "be careful. There are all sorts of demons here." She nodded her head and started her journey to Anubis.

Up in the air on Aten, Kepra could see that there were spirits one after another trying to get to the afterlife and some souls that could not pass because of grave crimes that they had done in their past life. For those who could not pass, they were gobbled up by the demon Amit. He was the devourer of the dead. Aten and Kepra, after figuring out how to get to Anubis, decided to take a shortcut and save some time. It was like a labyrinth in the underworld. They went along the outskirts seeing every inch of the place. Kepra told Aten to land; she could see Anubis from a distance. As they were walking, Kepra could see a shadowlike figure behind her in her peripheral. It began to get closer. She decided to turn around and take a look, but there was nothing there. Kepra, who was worried at this point, decided to keep walking. She had an eerie feeling with every step. She began to see the shadowlike figure getting closer. She turned around immediately with confusion written all over her face. She looked harder to see if she could make out what it was. She backtracked her steps to see what was lurking in the blight. As she continued looking, the dark silhouette appeared to be running toward her with inhuman speed. Kepra held her ground and saw a snakelike monster revealing itself approaching; she could feel the energy emitted. The force felt dark and demonic.

The creature struck out, trying to bite Kepra. Kepra leaped up in the air with her hands reaching for the beast's head and wrapped her hands around the beast's neck. The serpent continued to come to try and maul her. It possessed enough force that it eventually found itself breaking free of her grip. Kepra was stunned for a minute. Falling to the hard, cold ground, she shook off the attack while rising to her feet. Kepra focused on herself, took out her sword, and began to run toward the monster with it in her hand. She struck at the serpent, cutting only a small part of the snake. The demon let out a loud screech. The monster was gigantic. It had to have been at least ten feet in length. Every strike Kepra unleashed upon the beast, it would block her sword with its monstrous fangs. It had an immense amount of power behind every attack that was unleashed. Kepra kept trying to avoid the serpent's bite at whatever cost. She noticed that when he would lunge himself at her and miss that the drool coming from its mouth would disintegrate whatever it came in contact with. She knew that the venom dripping was not only poisonous, but it also produced pure acid. Kepra made a quick realization that the fangs in his mouth and the drool had to be avoided at whatever cost. There was no easy way out of this fight, she thought, and it was becoming dangerous. Acid was everywhere she looked, and the smell was making her nauseous. She noticed that the whole time the snake and her were fighting, he was trying to trap her by moving his body around the two of them. She knew if he succeeded in surrounding her, he would try to wrap his body around her and constrict and devour her soul.

Kepra looked around. She quickly noticed Aten pacing back and forth. He looked worried. She called out to Aten to come to her aid. He jumped over the snake's scaly body and scooped her up. Kepra hopped on Aten and began flying. She had formulated an idea that would put the monster in a position where she could finally kill it. Aten and Kepra flew throughout the underworld. The creature, wanting nothing more than to get to Kepra, followed with ease. Kepra was relieved that the snakelike monster took an interest in keeping up with them. Her plan had worked. Kepra thought that if she could get the creature to follow her in and out of certain sections of the underworld, it would eventually tie itself up in a knot. Kepra looked back with the snake still on her back.

She continuously kept her eye on him, looking back until the creature came to an abrupt stop. Kepra turned around and saw the monster had finally got to the point of becoming a celtic knot. She giggled at the beast and approached its head that had fallen to the ground.

She got off Aten and looked the beast straight in the eye and said, "you thought you could beat me, huh?" She grabbed one of the lamps that was within reach. She then poured the lamp fluid in her mouth and grabbed a stick of wood nearby while quickly lighting it with another lamp that was in short distance. Kepra then blew at the fire on the stick with the fluid flying out of her mouth while igniting the fluid from her mouth, causing a combustion of fire to be used as a blowtorch. The creature cried out in pain and fell to the ground. His body was black and roasted, and the smell of burnt carcass was in the air, along with sounds of the body sizzling. Kepra then pulled out her sword and struck it completely through the middle of the serpent's head. Kepra took a step back to catch her breath when she noticed everything was cremated except for the two dangerous fangs she noticed during the battle. She took them from the fire, carefully wrapping them up with some of the cloth that she kept in the saddlebag on Aten. She then placed the items in the saddlebag and shut it.

While Kepra was putting the fangs in the bag, she remembered that Ptah lived in the underworld and decided she would visit him to see if he could take the fangs and turn them into something magnificent. Kepra hopped back on Aten and then continued her journey to the god Anubis. Kepra had lost sight of Anubis with all the chaos that happened with the demon. On the ride there, Kepra kept pulling out the fangs and looking at them. She began to visualize herself fighting with them. She thought about her mission to Anubis then looked back at the fangs. She thought that Anubis could wait just a while longer for her while she sought out Ptah. Kepra, barely remembering anything as a child, tried her best to envision the route to Ptah but couldn't. Kepra then thought of how all the other gods got around and wondered how she could teleport like them. She remembered seeing the gods do it a thousand times. They would close their eyes think of where they wanted to be, and... Before Kepra could open her eyes, she heard the clinking of Ptah blacksmithing weapons.

She opened her eyes looked around, but still not seeing anyone, Kepra only heard the sound of the weapons being made. She stepped off Aten and started walking around the place when a voice startled her. "Hello, Kepra. What brings you here?".

She smiled and said to him, "it worked. It worked." As she continued to laugh and smile, he asked her what the celebration was about. She then told him she had never teleported before, let alone an animal the size of Aten. She walked back over to Aten to retrieve the fangs and show Ptah. Kepra turned to him and asked he had ever seen anything like it as she unfolded the cloth from the items. Ptah was a creator god; he made all sorts of weapons from scratch, but he would only fire up his pit for the gods. A normal blade, arrow, et cetera, could never kill a god. If Ptah himself did not construct it , it could kill no god. He looked over it for a moment noticing the fangs still releasing fumes. He asked the young warrior where she acquired the teeth, so Kepra began to tell him about the battle between her and the demon on her way to see Anubis. His face went into shock as she explained the battle in detail. He looked at her for a second and asked if she was hurt or if she needed need anything.

Kepra laughed. "no. Besides a few scrapes and bruises, I'm fine. I am a warrior now, Ptah; I am no longer a child," she said as she rolled her eyes. Kepra looked at Ptah. He still seemed to look worried. "Ptah, is there something about the demon that I should know? You looked troubled," she said.

Ptah asked Kepra to sit down as he told her the story of the demon. After sitting down, Ptah blew out a sigh, and he put one of his hands on his forehead, massaging it as he began. "Where do I begin, little one?" He said. He told her the demon she battled with was Apophis, and he had been haunting the underworld for centuries. Many had tried to stop him, but no one had ever been able to. He then stopped massaging his forehead and looked down at the floor. He went on to tell her it was also her mother's child. Kepra was confused with an eyebrow raised.

She asked, "so I technically just killed my sibling?".

He answered, "yes, but he was the epitome of evil. It was far more evil than set himself." He told her to ask her mother or Anubis. Once seeing him, she complied and said OK. They got up from their seats and moved closer to the fangs once again. "What do you think about the fangs? Is there a weapon to be made out of them?" She asked.

"Kepra, my dear, you forget who you're talking to. I'm the god of weapons. I can make a weapon out of a piece of hair." Kepra mentioned the venom that was coming from the fangs. Ptah looked and, while examining it, said, "this is going to come in handy. I can use the venom to add to the weapon's strength and abilities." Ptah told Kepra he could manufacture this weapon, but it would take some time. The earliest it could be done would be a fortnight.

Kepra said all right and told him she had previous engagements with Anubis anyway. She told him after the meeting with him, she would come back to check on the finalization of the weapons. He agreed and said that it should be done by then.

She thanked Ptah and headed on her way. Before she could reach the door, Ptah told her to wait and asked for some of her blood. The goddess looked confused and questioned him. "Why would you need my blood, Ptah?".

The god looked at her and said, "I apologize if it sounds weird, but it is to make the weapon customary to you and you alone. A blood bond binds you to the weapon for all of eternity. If anyone were to get a hold of the fangs, they could not harm you if I coat the weapon with your blood.".

The warrior agreed and thanked him again and set out on her quest with Aten behind her. When she left out Ptah's quarters, she then remembered she could just transport herself near the front of the line to see Anubis. She hopped on the lion and closed her eyes. She thought only of Anubis and even said his name aloud.

Before Kepra knew it, she was in from the jackal god with nothing more than a bat of an eyelash. She was in the hall of two truths, the weighing of the soul. She had finally made it to the god of the undead, but to her dismay, he was too busy to step away from his duties. He called upon Osiris to stay at the front of the line. Once doing that, he called upon Hathor, the mistress of the west. Hathor was to take Osiris's place and greet the souls once they arrived in the underworld. Anubis, finally getting things in order, took Kepra around and ask her how her journey was in Duat.

She looked around in wonder and said, "it was fine, all except running into a demon that tried to take my head off.".

He looked at her and asked, "what demon are you talking about, little one? There are millions in this world.".

As they walked alongside each other, she explained to him that it was a snakelike figure, and before arriving at him, she had met with Ptah, who told her that the demon's name was Apophis. Anubis's eyes were wide in shock. She said, "yeah, I know. Ptah sort of gave me the same look that you're giving me right now.".

He looked at her and switched his facial expression to one that was more relieved and happier. "No, no. Congratulations for beating such a demon. You are just so young to be displaying such great power already, Kepra. I'm impressed and relieved you are not hurt.".

Kepra stopped dead in her tracks, turned to Anubis, and asked, "why does everyone keep thinking that I'm still this little girl? Everyone even still calls me little one. I'm eighteen now, and people still treat me as if I'm some delicate flower. Well, I'm not!" She shouted. "I'm a warrior, one of the best warriors in the kingdoms.".

Anubis looked apologetic. "I'm sorry, Kepra. I think the reason behind it all is we have seen you so young not too long ago. Most of us have been around since the beginning of time. It is no disrespect nor to demean you, I assure you. We are just much older. I will not use it again, though, if it makes you feel less than the great warrior that you are.".

"I understand. I'm sorry for yelling at you, Anubis. I'm just going to have to prove to the gods that I am not the young goddess anymore that they once knew. I am a grown woman, and one day, I will show all the gods.".

Kepra and Anubis continued walking after she had cooled off. Anubis said, "Apophis is definitely a formidable foe, though. I am very proud of you. He has been a menace to the Duat for almost as long as I have been alive." Anubis stopped and looked off into the distance as if he were trying to reminisce. He told Kepra that he also had a story to tell her of the demon's wrath. He began to tell her the story of the elder Amun-ra. How he would lift the sun and travel into the depths of the underworld until the sun was to reach its peak every morning, and during that event, he would meet with the awful demon serpent, Apophis. Thoth would also accompany him in his journeys. Apophis was sought to kill the great god Amun-ra and prevent sunrise every night but never truly achieved his goal. Anubis told her that the great Amun would be overwhelmed about hearing that the monster had finally been laid to rest. Amun would no longer have to fight every night to try and get the sun into the heavens.

Kepra couldn't believe that she had done something that would make a difference to the gods. She felt she was on the way to making a name for herself other than little one. After the heavy conversation that Anubis and Kepra encountered, she told the god that the demon possessed very poisonous fangs and that she picked them up after burning the body to a crisp. Her delay was not to ask the god Ptah about the demon but to manufacture a weapon of unique origin for her. Anubis was once again feeling proud of her for thinking of making a weapon from a fallen enemy. Anubis assured her if anyone could make something powerful out of nothing, it was Ptah.

Kepra and Anubis continued to walk through the gloomy trail that looked out into the underworld. Kepra noticed from where they were standing that not only were the souls just coming from all over the place. A ferry was also carrying souls, taking them to Hathor, where the pathway to the two truths started. The lake was completely black. The only way of seeing the ferry throughout the darkness was via the lamps that were decorated around the Duat. Kepra, walking in front of Anubis, getting in all of the sights, heard a whistle from behind her. It was Anubis calling out for his horse. A beautiful, majestic creature appeared in from out of the darkness. The beast's main tail and fur just above the hooves were on fire. The horse itself was a black beauty. Kepra looked at Aten, then at Anubis. "Why are you calling for the horse, Anubis?".

"Let us leave the lion for a moment to see if we can make you remember anything about the Duat from childhood by riding around," he said.

She looked at Aten. He raised an eyebrow as if confused. She said, "what about Aten?".

"We will teleport back here when we are done. No harm shall come to him. You have already slain the deadliest monster in the underworld." He laughed." trust me," he said as he reached for her hand to hop onto the horse.

She took his hand and got onto the horse. She looked at Aten and said they would be back shortly. Aten shook his head in agreeance with her. Kepra, Anubis, and the fire beast took off with great speed into the darkness. They zoomed in and out of the underworld's labyrinth, trying to jog Kepra's memories. Anubis was patient with her, though. Memories she could not remember he would tell her the significance of each stop. He told her stories of how Neith would bring her here, and she would run around without a care in the world. Kepra looked at him and saw the smile run across his face. "what's with the sappy look, Anubis?" She said.

"it's just even as a child, you were tough as rock. You were adorable. You would pick up things half your size. We all knew you would be something special, Kepra," he said as he looked into her eyes. "it's just your destiny to find out what that special thing is.".

Their final destination had finally come. They ended their journey where they began at the hall of truth. Anubis explained the souls either go to the fields of reeds or are judged and stay in the underworld. He told her, "We believe that the souls reside in the heart, and so, upon death, the soul walks to the end of the path to the hall of truth, where the weighing of the heart occurs." When Kepra and Anubis got closer, Kepra saw a huge scale with an Ibis feather on one side and a heart on the other. The feather belonged to one of her loves, Thoth. Kepra also saw when the souls approached, Anubis's daughter qebhet would comfort them with the personification of cool, refreshing water.

Kepra also saw other goddesses there to help—Nephthys and Serket and the goddess that protected the souls of the dead. Kepra got a little closer, and Anubis interrupted her gaze by saying, "when it becomes one's turn, I am usually leading the soul to stand before Osiris and the scribe of the gods, whom you know as your friend Thoth. We walk the soul up in front of the golden scales. The goddess Ma'at would also be present, and these gods would be surrounded by the forty-two judges, who would consult with these gods on one's eternal fate. If the hearts were filled with goodness and lighter than the feather, they were to go to the fields of reeds. If they were filled with evil and their hearts weighed more than the feather of truth, then the scale would tip and fall into the crocodilian jaws of the demon Amit.".

Kepra had seen all she could learn for the day and decided to take off to revisit the god Ptah to check on the revamped fangs she left with him to forge. Kepra asked Anubis if he could teleport her to Aten so that she could be on her way. He nodded, and they walked back to the fiery horse. Anubis and Kepra hopped on the horse and then appeared in front of Aten once again in seconds. Kepra was relieved that he was still there and in one piece. Anubis laughed as he helped her off the horse and said, "you thought something was going happen to the great Kepra's beast?".

Kepra snatched her hand away from him. She felt as if he were mocking her. Kepra walked to Aten, rubbed his head, and hopped on him. Before Anubis left, Kepra remembered that her mother requested her to ask Anubis about the lives of two mortals. "Anubis, before you leave, I have a favor to ask from my mother," she said.

Anubis looked confused and said, "ok. What, pray tell, may the favor be, goddess.".

She looked at him in confusion herself and said, "honestly, I don't get it, but it was about two mortals on earth. She wanted to know when she would expect them to be in the book of the dead? She said you would know of whom I speak.".

"I do. Tell your mother that the two should depart to the underworld when the dead arises, and that is all.".

Kepra, more confused at this point because of the poem Anubis just tried to give her, cared less and told him she would tell her. Kepra thanked the mighty god and said goodbye. Anubis said farewell and rode off on his beast. Kepra yelled after him, "the great Anubis, why do you need a horse? You can teleport, you know?".

She could hear him faintly respond to her smart remark. "that's the problem with new gods. They never learn the old ways," he said as he disappeared into the darkness once again.

A fortnight had passed, and Kepra returned to Ptah. The nights seemed endless and like seconds in the underworld. Kepra hoped that Ptah would be finished by the time she got to him. Kepra remembered how she got there last time by closing her eyes, she thought of Ptah, and tried to fixate her nose to how the weapons smelled being forged, and just like that, she appeared. Kepra immediately heard Ptah's voice say, "hello, Kepra. I wondered when you would be back.".

"Yeah, sorry, Ptah; I lost time in the underworld. It is not like in Aaru. It's a lot to get used to, you know?".

Ptah walked over to where the fangs were and brought them back for Kepra to see. She was stunned. Excitement overtook her as she reached out to touch the gift that Ptah had put together. The weapon was beautifully designed. The fangs were made into a double-sided knife bent just enough to be used as a boomerang but came apart for her to use as two daggers. In the middle of the fangs where the grip lain was a lion roaring with a sun behind it. The two fangs that stood all alone before were now the opposite. They were the color green due to the venom that was seeping out from them. They were deadly, but due to the advanced overlay, Ptah had coated the fangs so they could not harm the goddess. Ptah explained this to Kepra, and with excitement in her eyes still, Ptah placed the weapon in her hands. Kepra's hands gently rubbed over every inch of the fangs in admiration. While Kepra was examining the fangs,

Ptah took a holder for the fangs off his wall of many intriguing weapons. He told her, "Use this to contain the weapon. It should stop the venom from penetrating your armor.".

She nodded her head and placed it on the side of her. Next, Ptah wanted to see how she handled the newly forged weapon. He asked her if they could leave Aten there and go somewhere to try it out. She agreed. Ptah grabbed her hand. Kepra gave Aten a look that signaled "I'll be back again." Kepra felt bad for leaving her companion again, but she knew he understood, and he was in a safe place. Kepra looked back at Ptah, and he told her to close her eyes, and with a blink of an eye, they were off.

Ptah took Kepra to a place on earth that looked as if it were made specifically for training an army. It looked so old and run down. There were arrows, skeletons, and swords everywhere. Kepra looked up after examining where they were and asked what the place was. Ptah looked at her and saw her face in confusion. He knew she was wondering why they were at an old rundown fort. Ptah looked around at the place while saying to her, "it is where I come whenever I want to figure new weapons out. It allows me to do whatever I want with the weapon without destroying anything or anyone. At my own free will here, no one would ever come to a deserted army base.".

"So—".

"Hush now, Kepra, no questions. Let's do what we came to do and see if you can use that thing," he said. She took the fangs out of the holder and noticed they were not glowing. She was confused. Ptah told her the holder controls the fangs. "When you do not need them, they go dormant." He also told her the fangs could only become poisonous with her activating them.

She scratched her head. "How do I do that?" She asked him.

He told her, "It's just like warping to another place; think of the green poison. Now picture it inside of you; picture that energy flowing through your body into your hand and onto the fangs.".

She could feel it. Her body was surging with energy; she felt more powerful. When she opened her eyes, the fangs were glowing green. She had successfully activated them. Kepra threw them one time, and they hit a rock and swooped completely around. She reached one hand up in the air to catch them. Once she successfully caught them, she stared at there for a second and then focused her gaze on Ptah. "they're awesome, Ptah. The power that they possess is unreal. Thank you so much.".

He said, "don't thank me yet. We still have more training to do. You must be able to handle them in all of their forms." Ptah looked around and focused his attention inside the fort. Kepra and Ptah walked inside the huge stone structure that once was a stronghold for armies. There was grass and plants everywhere. You couldn't see anything because of the height of it. Ptah saw a sizable opening that was coming from the top of the fort that surrounded its entirety. Ptah looked at Kepra to keep following him, and they started heading in its direction. Ptah and Kepra finally got to the middle of the fort. Ptah looked around and then looked at Kepra and said, "can you tell I haven't been here in a while?".

Kepra rolled her eyes and then left her eyes on Ptah. Ptah waved one hand, and everywhere the sun touched, the weeds were completely gone. "I wish you would have done that before we walked through all that shit," Kepra said under her breath.

Ptah looked at Kepra and asked her, "did you say something, Kepra?".

"Oh, I was just saying that was pretty cool how you just did that so quick," Kepra said as she rolled her eyes again once he looked away. Ptah was standing some ways away from the goddess when he eliminated the tall weeds. Ptah walked toward Kepra as he got closer to her. He told her he would spawn figures to kill with the daggers, to see how she dealt with the new weapon in combat. She agreed to the lesson without hesitation. She was excited.

She took out the fangs and held them tight in her hands and looked at him and said, "I'm ready.".

He was just about to snap his fingers for the figures to appear. He stopped, and she quickly looked at him, noticing his hesitation. "Kepra, there is one more thing you should know. They can kill you if you let them. I am not going to stop that. Both of us know you are one of the best warriors in the galaxy. So please don't disappoint me, or we're both dead.".

She stayed focused like she didn't care about what he just said. She said again, "I'm ready, Ptah.".

Ptah snapped his fingers and made fake humans appear out of the grass Ptah left surrounding them. "Kepra!" He screamed. "As soon as they hit the ground, they will disappear.".

She narrowed her eyes and concentrated on them. They were running through the tall scrub of grass like animals coming straight for her. With one more glance at them, she turned her body all the way around and flung her body, releasing the fangs in a perfect line to one of the men. There were five men. Kepra's fangs hit one and then continued to hit one man after another. She hit all five in one throw. She jumped up and down in excitement at defeating them. Ptah congratulated her and told her she had one more test. She calmed down and became serious, she focused her attention on the task at hand again. He told her, "This time the opponent will be in close quarters with you. The person will not die until you strike him with the poisonous blade and infect him.".

Kepra understood. Ptah spawned another human, and this time, he was right in front of her. The imitation human pulled out his sword before he could swing. Ptah yelled out, "oh, and Kepra, he's much harder to kill than the previous ones.".

She shot a look at Ptah that could have killed. The imitation human was about to strike when Kepra blocked his attack with her hands. She caught the sword in the middle of her palms and forced it out of the spawn's hands. She took out her sword and started fighting. While she was fighting, Ptah spawned more imitation human warriors. She was surrounded. Kepra, in the middle of all the warriors, jumped backward out of the circle and unsheathed her fangs. She threw the fangs out into the distance. They hit a rock and separated. Kepra's face looked shocked, and she didn't know what happened. The fangs that had split were still going. Kepra concentrated on the men in front of her and kicked one in the chest, making him fall to the ground. The other four quickly surrounded her. Kepra looked around. She could hear the fangs getting closer. Kepra had no idea what the fangs were going to do now that they had split. While Kepra was busy looking around, the warriors decided to strike at the same time. Kepra flinched and closed her eyes, seeing the warriors about to attack, when all of a sudden she looked up. Every one of them had been beheaded by the poisonous fangs. Kepra took a sigh of relief and saw that the fangs came back together after killing the warriors. Kepra lifted one hand in the air, and they fell right into her palm.

Ptah was impressed. He walked over to her and told her, "The training is completed. I am sure you will do wonders with these by your side, Kepra.".

Kepra hesitated walking with Ptah at first due to the confused thought of why the fangs separated. "Ptah," she asked, "why did the fangs separate?".

He looked back at her. Kepra was still in the same spot where she had finished her battle. He walked back to her and said, "Kepra, these fangs go where you want them to go." Ptah put his hand on Kepra's back, nudging her to walk alongside him as he explained in more detail. He continued. "The fangs feel your energy and your energy alone, so if you want to kill multiple people at once and see the vision in your head, the fangs fulfill the request that goes through your mind. So, in other words, even when you do not know how you are going to do it, fling the swords. They will handle it.".

"They're like magic," she said.

"Aren't all gifts from the gods, Kepra?" Ptah said.

She graciously thanked him again for the fangs. Ptah said one more thing before grabbing her hands and returning to his lair. "You will be able to fight with the fangs as if they were daggers. They will come apart and reattach at your will, Kepra," Ptah said. She shook her head in understanding. Ptah grabbed her hands. Then the two disappeared back to the Duat.

Aten quickly ran over to Kepra and stood up on two legs to try and hug her. "whoeeeeee, I missed you, buddy," she said as she laughed. "Have I been gone that long, Aten?" She asked. Kepra looked at Ptah and thanked him once more for all the effort he had put into the fangs. They were indeed legendary. He told her she was welcome and the pleasure was all his. While walking out, Kepra reassured Ptah if he ever needed her, she would definitely be there. He thanked her, and Kepra and Aten went back into the Duat once more.

Kepra decided to teleport just before the field of reeds. She wanted to fly in, seeing the beauty of it all after being in such a glum place. Kepra closed her eyes and imagined seeing the palace from a distance, and just like that, she appeared in the clouds looking at the exact thing she wanted to see. Aten and her flew toward the palace. Kepra saw the golden gates and the gods who protected it. Kepra and Aten fly in, seeing the ethereal heavens. Kepra had seen it a million times, but it always just seemed so magical to the eye. The waterfalls that were coming down off of buildings stopped right after the clouds. The flowers looked so beautiful with their massive size. There was also greenery everywhere, with white blossoms on the vines and trees. Twinkling sparkled from the pollen off

the plants. Gold brick decorated the roads connecting everything in Aaru.

Kepra got closer to the palace. She could see something was
stirring. It seemed as if all the gods were in attendance. Kepra
landed Aten and walked into the celebration.

Chapter 4
Uncertainty

Word had gotten back to the gods already of Kepra's great victory, beating the demon Apophis. Kepra could not believe that the defeat of the beast Apophis had reached Aaru already. Before approaching everyone, she saw banners of congratulations and whispers of where she was. Kepra could only think of one thing she could be celebrated for. Kepra looked at Aten and said, "I guess we are to be celebrated today, huh, boy?".

She and Aten walked over to the courtyard to get more details on what was going on. As she walked closer, she could see that every god was in attendance. "Beating Apophis must have been a great deal, Aten," she said as she looked around. The courtyards were tapered in vines and plants, and the courtyard ponds that were as deep as pools had white roses on the tops of them. Kepra, finally finding her mother amid such chaos, asked her mother what was going on. Neith had said, "for having beaten the beast Apophis, we celebrate your glory, darling. Amun himself had tried to defeat the creature for centuries.".

Kepra looked around, and everyone was celebrating her. She smirked and took a glass carried by one of the human souls working for the party and put it in the air to thank everyone for attending the event.

Amun came over to the warrior after the grand toast and told her, "I want to thank you for the hours that you have saved me.".

She looked at him confused and said, "what do you mean?".

He said, "I have tried from the beginning of time to defeat that monster. It seems you have done something that I couldn't. The nights will be more peaceful now. Delivering the sun through the underworld will not be a hindrance any longer. It will be a smooth transition from the sun to the moon and the moon to the sun because of you.".

She thanked the great god. She said to him, "the way you thank me is as if you know something I do not, great Amun.".

Amun looked from her out into the party and said, "every test is to make you who you are, young warrior goddess. It was meant for you to beat the beast, Kepra; it was your challenge alone. What did you obtain from it, goddess?" One of his eyebrows lifted, and she looked at him, and he looked at her.

Kepra said, "you knew I would get these teeth from the monster, didn't you?" He looked back into the crowd. "You also knew I would remember Ptah being in the Duat and seek him out to forge a weapon for me.".

He smirked and said, "enjoy your accomplishments, young warrior. You still have much to learn." She looked at him, smiling, and he at her as he walked away.

Kepra walked away and continued to celebrate with all of the gods. Kepra looked around. Horus approached her and started conversing. They were giggling and flirting with each other as usual. Hathor, who was in the distance, couldn't take anymore. She was tired of the spell-bound look he gave in public around Kepra. Hathor was certain that Horus was meant to be her mate, not an inferior goddess like Kepra. Hathor, among very few of the gods, did not like Kepra. Hathor thought Kepra was arrogant and naive. Rumors among the gods had it that Kepra was born from a human woman and that Neith killed another god, and by doing so, giving that godhood to Kepra to bring her to Aaru to sustain her immortality. Kepra was unaware that she wasn't born of a god. She was still living off the lie that Neith told her, that she was born from her. Kepra knew nothing more, nor did Neith allow such rumors to pass through her daughter's ears. No one was supposed to reveal the truth. Hell, no one knew the real truth, but Hathor had other ulterior motives. Even though Hathor did not have all the information on Kepra's birth, Hathor decided to make it seem like she did. She wanted to rip Kepra's heart out right there in front of everyone, making even her loyal friends question her creation. Hathor's infatuation with Horus made her take fate into her own hands. Hathor thought even if Kepra didn't believe her, she would still make the goddess feel humiliated in front of her beloved. Hathor was excited to put her plan into motion.

She walked over tapped Kepra on her shoulder and said, "why are you dancing with the god of war? You know, he only pities you because he and everyone else here knows you were not born amongst us. You were not born a true god." Everyone heard the rude comment that Hathor said to her. The party had immediately stopped. Hathor laughed as she said, "don't you know you are of human blood? Neith gave you the godhood you possess.".

Neith ran to her daughter and looked at Hathor and said, "you're a lying bitch, Hathor" and slapped her. "How dare you speak to my child with such a fabricated lie?".

Kepra looked at everyone with a glance. Amun appeared out of nowhere and grabbed Kepra's hand. "Do not leave your party like this, Kepra. Forget what she was saying. It matters not.".

"Amun, pardon my departure from the grand party you and mother have thrown me, but I must take my leave to clear my head. I'm sorry." She took her hand away from his and took leave up the grand staircase leading back into the palace. Kepra walked around for what seemed like hours, then finally headed to her quarters. Kepra reached her bedroom. She undressed and sat for a while in her room. With all of the commotion Kepra forgot to tell her mother of Anubis words. Kepra thought to herself that every party that was thrown for her always ended up in disaster.

As she drifted into deep thought, she heard a knock on her room's window. She looked outside only to see Horus on his falcon flying below. Horus saw Kepra peek out of the curtains. He called out to her, "Kepra!" But she ignored him. Kepra had drenched her pillow in tears, she hadn't noticed due to her being in deep thought. The tears had fallen from her cheeks, drowning the plush material. She hated that she felt like Hathor might somewhat be right. She hated the notion of not quite feeling like she belonged in the gods 'world. Most of all she hated not knowing her origin. Kepra felt unloved. She felt a need and turning to disappear from this life. She thought there must be more out there than this pain she kept revisiting every day.

Kepra heard another knock on her window. Horus called out to her once more, and Kepra slipped her robe on over her lingerie. Kepra tried to open the window when her robe flew open as the wind caught it. She wiped her face from the tears and looked over the window and asked, "what do you want, Horus?".

He looked at her with lust in his eyes and told her, "Kepra, I'm sorry if you're hurt, and forgive me for the intrusion, but you are the most beautiful goddess I have ever seen. If you think that I would take Hathor the bitch instead of you, all that reading that bird boy is teaching you must not be getting into that head of yours, because you know nothing.".

Kepra smiled and said, "apparently, I am not a goddess.".

He said, "have you asked your mother? There is no way that you cannot be a god, Kepra. It's foolishness that Hathor is using to get into your head. A god cannot make someone a god unless there is the death of a god or the willingness of a god to give up his or her godhood to another. If everyone could be a god, don't you think Aaru would be filled with human souls trying to portray us?".

She looked at him and said, "you're right.".

Horus said, "I may look young, my love, but I have been a god for centuries and centuries. I know a thing or two, trust me. Hathor was just talking out of anger because she wants me, but everyone that can see knows that you are whom I desire. You're the one I want to be with, and you know that. Now let me inside, please," he said.

Kepra invited him in, and they slept the night away, bodies conjoined. Horus was mending her emotions and making everything seem balanced again. "Thank you for always being there, Horus; you mean a lot to me.".

The next morning Kepra awoke to Horus beside her. The two were engulfed in each other's energy. Horus leaned over and whispered in Kepra's ear, "hey, I have a surprise for you. Come on and get up." Horus had decided to take Kepra to the other side of Aaru and take a bath in the rainbow springs. Kepra got ready for the day with Horus, Horus took the sash from her robe and placed it around her face to hide her eyes to keep her completely surprised up until they're arrival. Horus then placed Kepra on Aten, and he got on behind her. He held her gently the whole way there, carefully not giving any hints to where they were going. Horus could see the springs in the distance. While Aten was preparing to land, he held Kepra closer and told her to trust him. He picked her up, and they jumped off Aten in the pool of springs.

Kepra yelled out with Horus taking her blindfold off in midjump. She smiled while he was taking it off and then yelled loudly just before their bodies hit the water. Kepra came up for air, panting, trying to catch her breath. Horus appeared next to her, laughing at the expression on Kepra's face. She splashed him with a swipe of water from her hand and yelled out, "jerk!" With a hard laugh. Kepra looked around and was stunned by the springs. The springs were beautiful. They looked like huge amethyst crystal bathtubs. Crystals aligned the entire spring floor. The crystals were shaved down so that the ground was not difficult to step on. There were bigger crystals that came out of the springs, but there were mostly for show and did not interfere with swimming. They seemed to be in just the right place for it to look celestial. There were smaller pools that ventured of from the main one. The pools were hazy, looking as if there were infused with something. Some plants and trees hovered over the springs along with beautiful flowers that Kepra had never seen because they did not grow on the other side of Aaru. Everything looked so magical. Horus and Kepra swam to one of the smaller pools to become more intimate. Kepra sank way down into the springs and thanked him for the spa day.

He said, "you deserve it after a night like that.".

"Why are the pools murky looking?" Kepra asked.

"Oh, I'm sorry, I should have told you it's milk and honey in the springs. It makes your skin incredibly softer," Horus said. Kepra's face seemed pleased. She was so relaxed her mind began to wander. Kepra sat there for a moment, and then she asked Horus if he knew of anything about her birth. Horus delayed his answer but reassured her he knew nothing about it. "Neith suddenly came to us one day and told us she had given birth. No one questioned her; we just accepted it. We knew you had to be a god because you wouldn't have been able to stay up here with us. So, no one thought anything of it. Life just continued on with Neith and her new baby girl, you," he said. "that's all I know, my love.".

She looked at him, thanked him, and looked off into the distance once again. He was worried about Kepra. He could see Hathor's words were eating at her. "Kepra," he said "if I may, you are way more of a god, goddess than anyone in the heavens. You pretty much can beat me in a battle. You always strive to outdo all of the gods when it comes to something you are passionate about. I've never seen such hunger in someone's eyes to be damn near perfect. You are a god, Kepra, and to hell what anyone else thinks. Remember that, ok?".

She looked back at him and moved closer to him. She placed her hands on the sides of his face and brought it closer to hers. She placed her lips on his, and their lips melted into each other.

The intensity between the two surrounded the springs, and a glow came from within the waters. It was a bright iridescent light. Kepra looked down fascinated and tried to grab the water, but it was just normal when she cupped it in her hands. Horus said, "the water is only activated when two people are in love.".

She looked at Horus and began to get mad. "You wanted to know if I loved you? That's the reason you brought me here, isn't it, Horus?" She said.

He shook his head. "No, I thought you would like it because it was magical.".

Kepra got out and whistled for Aten. He came down in a roar from the skies and picked her up. Horus tried to stop her, drying off while getting out of the spring, one foot hopping up and down to not fall from trying to put the clothes back on in a hurry. "You tricked me, Horus," she said, and with that, she flew back to the palace.

Horus flew behind her, trying to catch up, but it was of no use. Aten would not let Horus pass to get to her. Kepra got back to the palace and hopped back into her open window. Horus called out to her while she was almost inside. "I love you. I didn't do that on purpose. Please believe me.".

She looked back and then continued to close the window and curtains. Horus sighed deeply as he watched her image disappear. He turned around with his hand rubbing his forehead, his eyes in sadness. The night of romance that he had hoped for only lead to her being angry with him once again, but at least he knew one thing was for certain, something that she could not hide any longer. She was in love with him. The beauty from the rainbow springs doesn't lie, he thought.

The next day Kepra roamed the palace walls searching for her mother; she was calmer and levelheaded now to talk and deal with her emotions than before, but Kepra could not find her. Kepra looked everywhere. There was still no sign of her mother. Kepra decided to go to the library and see the god Thoth for some more information on her origin. She thought if anyone knew about her birth, it would be him, the all-knowing god of knowledge. As she was walking, Kepra could smell the awful stench of her enemy's love potion fragrance. Kepra was looking down when Hathor came out of nowhere and walked into Kepra on purpose. "Excuse yourself, wannabe. I'm walking here.".

Kepra looked at her for a minute and then shook her head back and forth. "I am not starting anything with you today, Hathor. Whatever reason you have to not like me is your business. I believe you are the goddess of love, right? Why don't you tend to your black heart? If you even have a heart, that is, before you try going for a man's heart that doesn't even acknowledge you exist when you walk into a room. You're pathetic if you ask me; you're way too old to be acting like a child that needs acceptance from a man." Kepra rolled her eyes as she walked off, while Hathor's mouth dropped, hearing the words from Kepra's anger.

Kepra walked to Thoth's library. She approached the large, vaulted area, and Thoth was doing what he did best: writing everything he knew that existed down for people who wanted to obtain his knowledge. From the beginning of time with Amun to up-to-date things that were currently happening in the cosmos. Thoth was not only the smartest existence in the whole universe. He was also looked at as the scribe for the gods. Kepra continued to go farther into the library without Thoth noticing. Kepra saw magic being done everywhere—books moving from shelf to shelf, and pens writing by themselves. It was amusing to Kepra. Thoth saw the goddess, and everything just stopped and dropped. It was as if Thoth couldn't concentrate on anything else but her. Kepra was standing there, with her kinky curly hair blowing ever so effortlessly in the wind coming in from the window. Her armor was snugging her hips and her breasts perfectly, and her eyes were pools of brown with little specks of freckles on her face. She was gorgeous. She was gorgeous without even trying.

She moved to the right quickly before the book in the air landed on her. When the items dropped, he came back to his senses and noticed he was staring at her. He glanced down and then back up at her and apologized for the mess. She giggled and told him that there was no need to apologize. He asked her what brought her to the old training lair. She looked around at all the books; there was an incredible number. There must have been over a trillion of them. She was sure he had added more to his collection since she had last visited. The library was massive. It was aligned with trinkets and globes and sculptures of some of the gods. He cleared his throat and said, "Kepra, is there anything I can help you with?".

She said, "yes, I'm sorry. Just feels like forever since I've been in this place." He looked at her and said, "I know. I remember when we used to—".

"Thoth!" She called out with embarrassment.

He said, "what? I was only going to say when we use to study all day until you memorized our history.".

She rolled her eyes, and he laughed. "Hey, Thoth about that. I was wondering, Hathor told me some really intentionally mean stuff the other day, and I want to know if it's true or was she just trying to get under my skin. Do you think you can help me?".

He looked at her and said, "right, I remember Hathor the bitch; yes, I remember that statement all too well. So, you want to know if you're a god? That is the question?".

She looked down with sadness in her eyes and said, "yes, that is my question. I want to know if I'm a real goddess. Am I even from here? I was trying to ask my mother today about the whole situation, but I can't find her anywhere in the palace.".

Thoth said, "Kepra, my dear, if I may ease your mind a little, you would not have been allowed in the realm of the gods unless you were dead or a god. We both know you're not dead, right?".

"Yes," she said, "I am not dead.".

"Well, then," he said, "I guess you have answered your question. You must be a god. Even the great god Amun himself cannot make anyone a god. It is only given to those who are born with the blood in their veins. The only other way would be someone taking a god's life force, and then giving another the god's power. A god would have to agree to give it up willingly. No god is going to give their life force to a human. There is nothing beneficial to the god." Thoth had begun putting the stuff up that was on the ground from when he was distracted by Kepra's presence and lost himself in the conversation. He noticed that he had done so by the awkward pause and felt like he was talking too much. He looked at Kepra and saw the confusion resting on her forehead and said, "Kepra, just know that you are a goddess, ok? I'm rambling now, and I feel like I was talking too much.".

"No, no, please explain more, Thoth," she said.

"The gods made the rule of making someone a god by giving them their life force to evolve us. That's why Amun is now Amun-ra. He evolved by taking ra and Amun to become the sun, the king of the gods. So rest assured, warrior goddess, she was only trying to get under your skin, ok? Probably just jealous that the falcon boy likes you.".

"Thoth, his name is Horus; I don't understand why you two can't get along.".

"We both love you, Kepra, and I feel like your heart leans more toward him than me. There will come a day when you have to choose, you do know that?" He said.

"What if I don't want to choose?" She said. "I like you both. You each give me something different, and I don't want to lose that or either one of you.".

"You are selfish, Kepra. That decision will be for Horus and me to discuss or fight about. More than likely fight to the death about.".

She gasped.

"Just kidding, Kepra," he said as he winked at her. Kepra walked over and stood in front of Thoth; she thanked him. Kepra leaned closer to his face and kissed him passionately. Thoth gratefully reciprocated the gesture by pulling her into him. He pushed her on the table that was next to them while kissing her, throwing all the items that were on it onto the floor. He paused and looked at the door. With just a matter of a thought wave, he locked it. Thoth turned his attention back to Kepra and began slowly taking her armor off, first her breastplate. He took his time kissing every inch of her while unbuckling it with his hands. Kepra ran her fingers through his black hair and led them all the way down his spine. Kepra's breastplate hit the ground with a loud thud.

Thoth cupped her breasts with his hands and brought one nipple to his mouth. Kepra moaned as he took to the second breast and licked that nipple. Thoth was doing all of this while still focusing on the armored skirt. It also found its way to the ground; Thoth kissed her down till he got to her belly button. He raised her legs and put them on his shoulders. Her feet rested against his back. He kissed further down past her belly button, where he began licking her. Kepra moaned in pleasure once more. He turned Kepra on her stomach and took her right there. He went slow and then sped up the pace. Their breaths and heartbeats were in sync. Thoth and Kepra finished at the same time, meeting each other in ecstasy. Kepra and Thoth kissed once more and then began getting themselves back together. Kepra put her armor on while admiring Thoth's beauty. His golden-brown skin was glistening from sweat. She hurried and looked away so that she wouldn't get caught staring.

"Kepra," he said as he straightened his garments, "that was possibly the best thing I've ever experienced. You are the most heavenly creation I've ever seen in all its vulnerability.".

She smiled. "You aren't so bad yourself," she said while lacing her boots back up. She turned around to say, "thank you for everything.".

He winked at her. "Anytime, love," he said sarcastically as he winked. She turned and walked out seductively and then vanished into the hallways of the palace to look for her mother once again.

Kepra wondered the palace hallways, trying to look for her mother, but there was still no sign of her anywhere. Kepra decided to walk outside to get some fresh air and take a moment to herself. As Kepra was descending the stairway leading to the courtyard, she saw her mother was sitting on a bench holding a colorful bird in her hand. Kepra walked slowly over to her and said, "hello, mother.".

Neith said, "hello, Kepra." Kepra asked her where she had been all day. "Kepra," she said, "unlike you, I have places to be and prayers to answer. I cannot be in the palace all day.".

Kepra said, "you won't let me go anywhere. That's why I'm stuck in the palace all day. You treat me as if I'm a child. I have trained for years practicing how to be the best warrior alive. I finally achieve it, and yet still you do not trust me to be out in the world by myself.".

Neith looked at her and said, "because you are not ready. You are the youngest among us.".

"Yes, but I am wise and stronger than almost anyone in the cosmos, mother. I do not need your protection any longer," Kepra said. Kepra blew her breath. "This isn't why I wanted to talk to you. What happened at that party, mom?" Kepra said.

"What do you mean?" Neith responded.

Kepra looked at her mother, who was still admiring the bird; Neith wasn't paying Kepra any attention. Kepra rolled her eyes. "Mother, you know exactly what I mean," Kepra said.

"Kepra, you are a full goddess. I am your mother. You have no father because I created you from a part of myself. That is your answer. Is it good enough for you; have I answered everything? By Amun, girl, you would think you would be smart enough not to believe everything gods say by now.".

Kepra shook her head and said, "I don't believe you!!," and stormed off toward the palace.

Neith yelled, "Kepra, Kepra, wait! Come back, please!" But Kepra ignored her and kept walking like she never heard a word.

Neith looked up to the skies and shook her head while saying, "Amun, help me with her." Kepra retreated to her quarters after leaving her mother in frustration. She was upset. Kepra felt like her mother was hiding something from her; she just couldn't figure out what it was. She was determined to get to the bottom of it whatever it was.

Chapter 5
A Visit

T he day finally came, and Kepra couldn't quite contain her overwhelming emotions. She was ecstatic. Her mom knew Kepra had been dealing with a lot, so Neith finally decided to take Thoth up on Kepra's birthday present and gave the ok to go to earth under the conditions of Thoth's papyrus. Thoth and Kepra were to dress like commoners and blend in with the crowd. They were not to bring any attention to themselves while among the humans. That was the deal Neith had made with the two before leaving for the mundane. Kepra awoke and put on a white and-gold kalasiris that was cut out on both sides. The stomach area also had a triangle cut along with two more cuts on each side that ran from her thighs to her feet. She wore golden jewelry from head to toe and makeup done in blues and blacks. She looked like a pharaoh returning to her kingdom to retake the throne.

After the soul servants were through dressing the goddess for her big day, Kepra sought out Thoth. Thoth was waiting in the courtyard for the goddess. Kepra approached the staircase that led into the courtyard. When Thoth saw the goddess, his mouth dropped, she blushed as she saw his face while walking toward him. When she got closer to him, she twirled around for him and asked if he liked the outfit. Neith had given it to her on the day of her birthday. Still in awe of the goddess, he said yes and told her she was the most beautiful thing he had ever seen. She thanked him and said, "we should hurry before my mother changes her mind." She grabbed his hand while giggling and headed to the gates of Aaru.

When they got to the gate, they took each other's hands, making eye contact. He said to her, "are you ready?".

She replied yes and then closed her eyes. Soon after, the two disappeared into thin light. When they had reached earth, it was like a hold on time for a second before they began to walk. A couple of seconds passed, and the people and noise resumed as if time had never been altered. Thoth took her by the hand and showed her the city of Pi-Ramesses. It was the new city Ramesses the great had built after the allegiance with the Hittites. The city stood for the house of Ramesses. It was the new capital of Egypt. Thoth showed the goddess every inch of the city to the palace where the pharaohs resided, to the temples where the people worshipped the gods, and even the marketplaces where Egypt's trade took place.

Thoth told the goddess to look around the marketplace and see if anything caught her eye. He said, "take your time, and I will return to you momentarily.".

She looked at him puzzled. "Where are you going, Thoth?" She said. He told her he had a present for her that he had to see about. She shook her head and said, "all right," and he disappeared. Kepra, lovely as ever, walked around the marketplace, viewing everything from food to golden artifacts. While she was walking around, she spotted a young man who didn't look at all like he had come to buy anything. He was ordering a lot of people around like he was someone of importance. He was dressed in armor that looked like the colors the pharaoh had in the palace. She was curious as to why everyone seemed to hold him in such high regard. While walking around, Kepra could overhear the people talking about the man. He was the commander in chief of the pharaoh's army. He was very pleasing to the eyes, and Kepra could not stop fondly staring. A few minutes passed of looking back and forth at him, and then suddenly, he saw her. Kepra saw him out of the corner of her eye gazing at her but pretended to be unaware. Kepra's hair was blowing in the wind, her body as if it was surrounded by light itself. He stood there for a moment like no one else in the world existed. She was stunning.

The man began walking over to her, passing everyone in his path, that was trying to get his attention. He couldn't look anywhere else. His eyes were fixated on the beautiful goddess. It was as if he were under a spell of some sort. He was drawn to her celestial beauty. While walking to her, he got interrupted by a guy walking completely in front of him. It was the general. He was yelling at the top of his lungs to get his attention. The commander finally broke free from the goddess. The general looked at him and said, "sir, are you all right?".

The commander shook his head as if to shake back into reality and said, "yes. Sorry, general, what were you saying again?".

The general told him important information that was passed down from the pharaoh; it was of the utmost importance that he hurry back to the palace. The commander nodded his head, but he looked for the woman before taking his leave. The commander needed to see the woman's beautiful face just once more. He looked in every direction hoping she would catch his eye, although it was nowhere to be found. He had never seen a face like that before. He began to question his sanity. Did he really see her? He wondered. Or was she just a figment of his imagination? He turned around and stood in the direction of the palace, trying to forget the ingrained image of the goddess.

The general looked back at the commander and said, "let's go, commander.".

He shook his head. "All right, all right," he said. "let's go." While leaving the market, the commander asked the general, "did you happen to see a long curly-haired beauty with skin as tan as the sands in the desert? I saw her, and then she just disappeared.".

The general looked at the commander and said, "no, commander. I saw no one but village women, no woman of what you speak. You must have seen a mirage from being out in the hot sun all day.".

"She was heavenly looking, general," the commander said.

"I'm sure she was, commander," the general said as he rolled his eyes. "Now let us hurry before the pharaoh has our head, commander." He popped the reins and made a sound where his tongue hit the roof of his mouth, signaling the horse to go much faster.

Thoth had pulled Kepra away in just that instant while the general was talking to the commander. Kepra and Thoth had arrived back in the heavens. Kepra looked at Thoth mad and asked, "why did you leave me for so long?".

He took a beautiful flower from behind his back and gave it to her. "I have designed these flowers for you, Kepra. I have made them on earth while we were there and brought the flowers here as well so that you may see them and think of me whenever you are in the heavens or on earth. They are called the blue lotus, the color of the eyeshadow that is placed on your brown eyes. They are a symbol of my love for you. It is your flower now." She blushed. He said, "I wanted it to be a surprise. That was the reason for taking you to earth.".

She smiled and then hugged him. She stayed in his arms and peered up at him. He took her chin in hand and pulled her lips close to him. They kissed with their tongues connected in a dance. "Thank you, Thoth.".

The night had just begun. Kepra took Thoth's hand and ran off with him into the palace. Before heading into the palace, you would first have to enter the courtyard. Thoth had placed the blue lotus everywhere in Aaru already. The flowers were massive in size and would fold up every time anyone went by them, all except for Kepra. Walking through the courtyard, Kepra noticed the blue lotus flowers floating on the pools in the courtyard. Some fireflies lit up the night skies. It was all so romantic. Kepra and Thoth were playing around near the pools, and Kepra pushed him in. He started laughing and asked her to come over to the pool. She shook her head no and said, "I know what you're going to try to do." He then made an illusion of himself that appeared behind her and pushed her in. She fell in and hit the water. When she came back up out of the water, she tried to splash the god.

He grabbed her and started kissing her. He began to kiss her lips all the way down to her neck. He paused ever so slowly in between kisses. He undressed her carefully in one motion, letting the dress float in the pool. Kepra, with nothing but her underwear on, felt Thoth's kisses moving down to her body and her temperature rising. All of a sudden, Kepra heard footsteps. They were getting closer by the minute. Kepra told Thoth to stop a moment and listen. Both in the pool of water stood perfectly still.

There were ledges around the pools that made it capable for them to hide just enough to remain out of sight. As the footsteps got closer, she could hear a familiar voice. It was her mother's voice, along with Bastet, talking about her. They stopped in front of the pool that was before the one Kepra and Thoth were in. Kepra could hear every word. Neith was telling Bastet that Kepra was asking a lot of questions lately about her birth, and she felt guilty for lying to her. Kepra, about to let out a gasp, was interrupted by Thoth's hands masking her mouth. He turned to Kepra and told her to hush. She nodded, and they continued to listen.

Bastet told Neith that she would eventually have to tell the truth. Neith, with tears streaming down her face, understood. Bastet walked over to Neith, put her hand on Neith's shoulders, and said, "in your own time, sister, in your own time." She thanked Bastet, and they both headed in the direction of the palace.

Kepra slowly peeped up out of the pool to make sure the coast was clear. Once completely out of the water, Kepra turned to Thoth and said, "you can come out. They're gone." She looked back and reached for his hand and said, "I knew something was off, and I knew she was lying. Thoth, what do I do now?".

While Thoth and Kepra fished their clothes out of the pool, he looked at her and could see Kepra's heart breaking. All of this just added more suspicion about her being a goddess. Kepra and Thoth began putting on their garments. Thoth looked down at the ground and told her, "I think you should go and visit the goddess, Isis. She is one of the oldest among us, and she and her power should be able to help you.".

"I don't think she likes me, Thoth.".

"Why?" He said.

"I don't think she particularly fancies that Horus likes me. I feel like she watches us.

Sometimes, she's overly protective.".

"Ohh, the falcon. Well, Kepra, I'm sorry to tell you this, but that's the only one that can probably give you the answers you need.".

She let out a loud sigh and said, "you're right; I'll see her tomorrow. Hopefully, she can tell me something of use.".

They were about to leave the courtyard and head back to the palace when Thoth stopped Kepra to tell her one last thing: "Kepra, don't let anyone know where you're going.".

She looked at him confused and said, "why not?".

He said, "I'm pretty sure if you told someone about it, they would know the reason of you going and might make it harder for you to see the witch. It will already be a difficult journey. The witch lives beyond the outskirts of Aaru.".

She nodded and said, "thank you for the advice." She then headed into the palace to sleep the night away. She was anxious about seeing the goddess Isis and what tomorrow's adventure might bring.

Chapter 6

Isis

As Kepra became older, she began questioning her mother more and more on why she could not visit the mundane by herself or at all for that matter. Her mother would always have excuses for her. She would tell her things like "you are not ready yet" or "you'll know when the time is right." Truthfully, Neith did not want Kepra to find out about her real parents or the real reason she could stay among the gods, but Kepra began to grow very impatient with the answers she kept receiving day and day out. Kepra felt it was time for her to take matters into her own hands. She could wait no longer.

The next morning, Kepra awoke. She began to think, and the more she thought, she began to get more upset. After so many months of trying to get information from her mother with no lead, Kepra put her foot down and finally decided to take the leap and visit Isis. Today was going to be the day she took an adventure to the beyond and see the oldest witch of all time. She was determined to get some answers, and she knew that Isis was the only one that could help her. Isis, the goddess of life and magic, who so happened to be Horus's mother. It was early, so early ra himself had not arisen yet. Kepra got dressed, put on her armor, and put Aten's saddlebags over her shoulder. Kepra grabbed her weapons just before walking out of her room, putting all of them on one by one, all while tiptoeing around each corner, trying to get out the front of the palace. Kepra made it to the last corner of the palace that she had to turn before the stairway to the court yards, and her heart stopped. She saw a black shadow by Aten. She was caught.

Kepra proceeded to walk toward Aten. She was not giving up that easily. As she got closer, she could see dark curly hair and muscles caressed in caramel chocolate. She exhaled in relief. It was the god of knowledge. Thoth awaited her outside in the courtyard. He was brushing Aten. He could see she was hesitant in approaching, not knowing who it was. As she got closer, Thoth turned around and asked her, "were you scared?" He giggled.

"Thoth," she softly yelled, "why were you trying to scare me?".

"I'm sorry, Kep. I just wanted to warn you. It's going to be really hard getting to Isis," Thoth said.

Kepra looked confused. "Why would you have to warn me?" She said.

"Do you even know how to get there?" Thoth questioned.

"I mean, I know the direction I should head in, if that's what you mean," Kepra said.

"Kepra, Isis is in the beyond. She's there for a reason. Do you know that reason? I never thought to teach you about her because I honestly thought she would never come up. She distances herself out there to not see us. She thinks she's better than us and that she should be in charge of the gods. So, when she finally got it through her head that none of us wanted her to lead us, she created her own space in Aaru but still separated from us. She still had followers that went with her. I'm trying to say that Isis is there because she doesn't want to be bothered by anyone. She has very few visitors, and the few visitors she does have live close by, so as not to get lost returning. On approaching the beyond and leaving Aaru, it will get foggy. You will become delusional. The path will no longer matter.

It is somewhere you can't just teleport. You will become lost, and then and only then will you find the beyond," he said.

Kepra said, "what? I will find the place when I am lost? Ok, well, that sounds sensible, Thoth.".

"Kepra, she has set up a barrier that challenges your sense of reality. Please just be prepared," Thoth said to her as he grabbed her by the arms.

"I will be fine, Thoth. Thank you for the concern, but there is no need to worry about me. I am Kepra warrior goddess," she said as she placed the saddlebags over Aten. She hopped on Aten and said goodbye to Thoth. Thoth waved to her till he could see her no longer. Kepra set out to find the wicked witch of Aaru.

Kepra's journey there was long. She was almost out of Aaru when she saw a massive amount of fog take over the skies. She was hesitant but knew she had to continue her journey. Kepra started to see the fog completely take over her and Aten. The fog became so thick that Kepra could no longer see her hand in front of her face. Kepra began to panic. She started hearing voices and seeing illusions. The voices became clearer and clearer. They were whispering her name, asking her to follow it. As Kepra got closer to the voices, an illusion began to appear. The fog started to separate, and the illusion became clearer to see. She couldn't believe it. She wiped her eyes to make sure her eyes were seeing correctly. It was Aten and herself. She felt Aten come to a stop. She looked down, but the fog was coming and going; it became hard to see again. All of a sudden, Kepra felt a slash on her arm. Aten reacted and began to start flying again; he picked up speed, trying to lose whatever it was attacking her.

Kepra could no longer see the illusion. She was confused. She thought, was the illusion the thing that cut me? All of a sudden, the illusion appeared in front of her. The blade that it was holding had blood dripping from it. It was Kepra's blood;

Kepra angrily grabbed her sword from its sheath and yelled out to Aten, "let's go! Aten, attack!" Kepra had not completely thought of how she would hit an illusion, but she didn't care. The illusion was trying to kill her, and she had to take it down before it got to her. She flew into battle with the fog still thick as ever. Kepra knew she would have to remember her training at this point. She closed her eyes and awaited the attack from the illusion. The illusion's sword was just about to pierce Kepra's stomach when Kepra hit the sword away with her sword. As soon as she hit the sword away, she hit the illusion in retaliation. The illusion became visible, and Kepra struck it again. The clonelike lion that the illusion was on shifted and took the illusion away from Kepra. Kepra went after it. The fog got thick again. Kepra had come to the conclusion that when she hit the illusion, the fog dissipated.

The more she hit the illusion, the more she could see. Kepra thought if she could kill the illusion that she could clear enough of a path to the beyond to reach the witch. Kepra closed her eyes and felt another attack about to happen. The attack was going toward Aten instead of her. The coward, she thought. The illusion is trying to hurt Aten to flip me off of him. Kepra quickly bent backward and stopped the illusions sword with her own. Kepra then got up on Aten and listened for the illusion to come closer to her. She flipped herself onto the lion of the illusion, the illusion got up, and the duel began between the two. Kepra, still barely seeing unless landing a blow against the illusion of herself, she had to rely on her ears alone in this battle. She sheathed the sword and released the fangs from her side. Kepra pulled the fangs apart and decided to use them as daggers because of their close quarters. The illusion kicked Kepra, making her lose her balance. With Kepra off-balance, the illusion took the opportunity to strike. Before, the illusion could hit where she fell.

Kepra had disappeared. The illusion looked over the side of the lion. Kepra had dropped onto the saddlebags. Unlike the illusion, Kepra had remembered that the saddlebags had feet placements that hung down low enough for Kepra to grab onto. This allowed Kepra to wait for the illusion to look over after thinking she had fallen to her death. Kepra swung her legs up and kicked the illusion off the lion while getting back on top. Kepra had defeated her illusion, and the fog started to disappear. The lion that had also been an illusion was starting to vanish. Kepra was desperate to find Aten. She looked all over for him. Kepra began to see her friend in far off distance, Aten appeared just in time. Kepra started to fall from the skies; she closed her eyes. The fog was no more; Aten quickly scanned the skies for Kepra. He came out of nowhere rescuing the young heroine. Kepra, with her eyes still closed, felt her body hit something. She had landed on Aten's back and let out a sigh of relief as she patted him on the back. "Good boy; I thought I was done for," she said as she laughed nervously. Now that the fog was gone, Kepra could see the witch's lair that was the beyond.

She and Aten carefully approached the beyond for fear of more trickery from the witch. There was a dock there. Aten and Kepra flew to it and landed. Kepra looked around as she was getting off of Aten's back. The air had gotten harsher, and the beauty had disappeared. It was a dreary place that almost looked creepy. She and Aten walked quietly to what seemed like a cave. As they were approaching, she could hear music coming from inside. Aten and Kepra kept walking along till they were outside the cave. When they approached the witch's lair, the music had gotten louder. The music sounded like flutes and running water with hints of chimes. Kepra could also hear voices coming from within. She could feel the energy that was seeping as it blasted its way out of the cave and through Kepra's body. An overwhelming feeling of lust came over her. She shook it off as she turned to Aten and told him to stay put. As Kepra entered the cave, chants and the sound of water flow became more prominent. The further she got, the more interesting the cave became. There were crowds of people having sex everywhere, switching every so often with other people in the room. There was a gray fog around everyone and everything that seemed like it was leading to something. It was if the fog was conducting them to move in this manner. There were candles lit all around, and incense burning that smelled like the goddess of love had made them herself. It was as if sex itself had embodied the first part of the cave. As Kepra continued to go further into the second half of the cave following the fog, she saw gods and goddess walking around naked, drinking wine, and conversing throughout the place. The fog led to a waterfall in the middle of the room. Kepra had found where the sound of water was coming from. Music still played throughout the cave, giving off an enchanting allure.

Kepra continued without hesitation as the ambiance of enticement filled the area. She walked more, and with every step, she became more at ease. It was a sudden urge of temptation that overcame her body. She resisted the urge of charm embodied from the cave and began to focus her attention on the task at hand: finding the witch. As Kepra got closer and closer to the goddess, Kepra noticed that all of the glamorous people who were once there had slowly started disappearing one by one. Kepra looked back and saw that the cave was empty—nothing more than a regular bleak cave. All of the people that she had seen before had mysteriously vanished. Kepra shook her head, and a rush of annoyance came over her; she was pissed at being tricked once again from the witch's illusions. Kepra approached the back of the cave slowly. It was the only place she had not checked for the witch. Isis saw Kepra approaching and came out of hiding by removing a sheer curtain that lead to her bed quarters. When Isis opened the curtains, she wasn't at all surprised to see Kepra; she knew what she was there for. Isis played ignorant and asked the young goddess what her reason for the sudden appearance was. "You have disturbed my little party, Kepra, my dear.".

Kepra's curiosity and awareness set in as she noticed the unbothered witch. "You seem so calm. Isis, why do you think I'm here? I have a feeling you've already been enlightened due to your lack of interest. Have you staged all this for me? Were you preparing for me, Isis? Awaiting my arrival?".

Isis walked over to the warrior. She leaned in closer to the goddess and said, "oh, but my child, you don't want to know all those questions; there is a more important question that you wish to know, isn't there?" Isis laughed menacingly.

Kepra took a step back and stared at the witch. "You have been wondering about how to get to this planet that was once your homeeeee, huh?" The witch said as she held up an illusion of the planet earth upon her palms. Kepra, in shock, mouth open wide, began to feel a wave of betrayal and confusion hit her body. Kepra knew she had always felt some sort of connection to the planet that Isis mentioned, and now she knew why.

Kepra asked Isis what she meant by saying it was her home. "I was born among the gods. My mother swore it, witch," Kepra said. " But what if this was all true? What if I am from earth?" Kepra said in her mind.

Isis began to tell Kepra all she needed to know. Isis formed gray matter into a huge ball, and from it poured Kepra's life. She told Kepra how her parents were nothing more than mere mortals who worshipped the gods and how they got into a situation that was way over their heads. Isis told Kepra of her parents 'great sacrifice. She told her that her parents gave her away to the one she called mother today, Neith, to save Egypt.

Kepra, with tears in her eyes, screamed in rage, "you're lying!" Kepra was devastated, her lungs filled up with air, and she felt like she couldn't breathe. She let out a piercing cry. Kepra couldn't believe all that she was hearing. "If that is all true, witch, then how do you suppose that I can remain in the palace of the gods, hmm?" Kepra said.

Isis agreed. "You are right, my child. That is a very good question indeed. One that even I can't answer for you." Isis dismissed the fog that was showing Kepra all its antiquities. She quickly moved closer to Kepra and hovered around like a vulture about to feast. "What are you going to do now, my dear? Everything you have known is a complete lie." Isis laughed.

Kepra stood there still in disbelief. Truthfully, she didn't know what she was going to do. She had a right mind to go back to Aaru and give Neith a piece of her mind. Kepra yelled, "you know nothing, Isis!" She yelled again on the way out. Kepra headed for the exit; she had gotten the answers she came for. She was tired of Isis mocking her; it was time to leave. It was time to get the whole truth. Kepra was on the way out when Isis grabbed her arm and said, "oh, but little warrior, before you go... There is something that you should know, I can make it so you can meet those pathetic parents of yours. Neith has made it so you cannot leave, but I can break that hold she has on you.".

Kepra, with tears running down her face, pulled away from Isis's grip, still confused. Kepra asked, "Isis, why would you help me? Your son is in love with me, and let's face it, I can feel your presence over us, watching us when we are alone together. You hate us being together.".

Isis reassured Kepra, "it is not that I don't like you, my dear. I just hate seeing my son with the likes of you.".

"What the hell have I done not to be worthy enough to be with your son?" Kepra asked.

"You make it impossible for Hathor and my son to be together; that is what you have done. You do not fit my son. Hathor has been molded specifically for Horus; you come out of nowhere with this arrogance, bewitching his mind with this notion of love. Nooooo, little one, that is my job, to cast the spells. I am not sure why you can live among us yet, but I will find out. My son deserves only the best, Kepra, my dear, and you are nothing more than a mere mortal playing a goddess," Isis said.

Kepra shouted, "I am a goddess! There is no way to fake that, and you know that, you senile old fool. A god cannot make someone else a god. They have to be born that way, and you of all people should know that, or is your lack of knowledge fading with being out here in this cave by yourself?" Kepra angrily tried to walk out of the cave once again.

Isis's voice echoed as she said, "Kepra, in a matter of moments, you can be on earth. I want you to disappear just as much as you want to explore this tiny little insignificant planet. With you gone, Horus will have time to explore his feelings with Hathor. You will no longer be in the way of their love. Why else do you think I would willingly give you all this counsel? Rejoin your true family, Kepra. There is no place for you here.".

Kepra immediately stopped walking and tried to hide her rage for Isis inside. Maybe I should; I have so many questions that can only be answered on earth, Kepra thought.

"So can we proceed?" Isis asked. "I shall now begin to bestow upon you the wish that you desire greatly. Oh, Kepra, there is one more thing. There is a stipulation to this spell.".

Kepra answered straight away, "yes, anything. What is it?".

Isis smiled ominously. "It will cost you... Your godhood.".

Kepra couldn't believe her ears. She looked down and around, trying to make a decision that would change her life forever. "By giving me the life force of a god or whatever it is keeping you in Aaru, you will automatically drop to Egypt. Oh, and another thing. You should know before going through with this you will never be able to cross into the underworld or Aaru again. But look at it this way: at least you can meet those parents of yours and have that mortal life you crave so much. Isn't that what you thirst for, Kepra?".

Kepra shook her head and finally made a conclusion. Kepra looked to her left and saw a magnificent mirror covered in gold accents and vines. The accents were hieroglyphs that depicted horns on top of a square and an x. They read, "open a portal from here to earth, a god no more, a human rebirth." Kepra stared at the gold hieroglyphs, and it seemed as if they were changing in size constantly as Isis recited the incantation. Kepra stared into the mirror for what seemed like forever to her. Her eyes felt heavy, and she could only think about Egypt. Isis had put Kepra into a trance, and Isis asked her, "what's it going to be, princess of Egypt?".

Kepra agreed with Isis. Isis made it hard for Kepra to make any other decision but go to Egypt. The trance Isis had put Kepra in left Isis with a smirk on her face. "Perfect! I knew you would see it my way." Isis got behind her in the mirror and told her to close her eyes. Kepra did as the witch commanded. She felt like her soul was being snatched from her body; she felt great pain, and then all of a sudden, the goddess awoke in a familiar place. It was Egypt.

Kepra had reached the alley just outside the market she had visited with Thoth. Kepra was dressed like a commoner. Kepra got up, examining herself carefully. She wasn't sure what just happened; she felt weak and still felt a slight tinge of pain over her body. She looked around and said to herself, "where the hell am I?".

Chapter 7
A Legend Is Born

I n the beyond after Kepra had disappeared, the loving animal that she had called her friend saw everything that happened between Isis and Kepra in the cave. Quietly tiptoeing back out of the cave, so as not to bring any attention to himself, Aten got outside the cave. He flew as fast as he could back to the safeness and protection of Aaru. When Aten had finally arrived, he immediately sought out Kepra's mother. Aten flew up the palace stairs straight to Neith's room, bursting through her bedroom doors. He whined and whined some more, trying to tell her to come with him.

"What are you trying to tell me, Aten? Neith noticed that Kepra wasn't with him. Where is Kepra?" Neith asked. Aten flew under Neith and got her to sit on him. Aten took off out the window to the beyond where Isis lived. When Neith got to the cave, she could feel that Kepra had been there; she jumped off and rushed to see the witch. Neith took Isis by the garments and hemmed her up, questioning her about Kepra's whereabouts. Isis laughed at Neith's aggressive interrogations and then proceeded to tell her that Kepra was where she found her so long ago.

"don't you remember, dear sister?" Isis said. Neith dropped the witch on the floor and thought for a moment.

Neith gasped. "You sent my child back to Egypt?" Neith said.

"Well, yes, that is where you wouldn't let her go, after all." Isis snickered.

"Where is she, Isis? Where in Egypt is she?" Neith questioned.

"That I do not know. She does not have her godhood any longer, so unless she seeks out help from one of the gods by praying, I'm not sure you'll ever find her." Isis laughed maliciously. "What do you mean, she doesn't have her godhood any longer? Isis, I will—".

"Now, now, dear sister, you wouldn't hurt your own family, would you? Your daughter damn near begged me to take it. Maybe if you had given her more freedom, you wouldn't be having this little problem," Isis said sarcastically. "I took her godhood; that was the only way she could go without you finding her and having to come back if you did," Isis continued.

"Isis, what have you done? Amun will hear of this, and I pray that you are banished from all Aaru when he finds out," Neith said with tears running down her face. She walked out of the cave and back to Aten. Aten could feel the sadness from Neith. He, too, was in agony. The two set out to Amun; when Aten and Neith got to the palace, Aten sat her down by the courtyard. She sat on a bench in front of a pond looking at the blue lotus that Thoth had made for her. Neith was so depressed and mad at herself for not telling Kepra about the situation before now. Neith sulked, thinking she could have stopped her beloved child from giving her life force away.

Eventually, word got out about Kepra's disappearance. When everyone heard about what happened, they were struck with grief. At this point, no one knew where she was or what anyone could do about it. Kepra had given her godhood away to the goddess Isis, and Isis wasn't departing from it that easily. If a god or goddess lost their immortality, they would lose it for eternity, never to see the beauty of Orion's belt again unless they were able to get ahold of the immortality they had lost.

The only way to get Kepra back to being a god was to take the bottle that it was contained in and find Kepra to return it to her. Neith feared that Isis would think that everyone in the kingdom would come for it now; she was sure that Isis was too smart to leave it around. Amun only knew what she could be doing with it. Neith cried, and Amun shook his head in disbelief, mad with anger. Still, he was not giving up on the young goddess that easily. Neith had other plans. Neith would surely make Isis pay for the betrayal of deceiving her daughter.

Amun hugged Neith and looked at her and told her not to worry. "It is foretold that a woman of warrior blood will ascend into Aaru and save all of humanity. This is her time now, Neith; she must have faith in herself because what is to come will not be easy.".

Isis had taken apart of Kepra, her godhood was half of who Kepra was. Before Isis disposed of Kepra in the mundane, she relinquished Kepra of all of her powers when she took her goddess essence. Isis had more evil motives than just getting rid of Kepra for the romantic relationship she had with her son. Isis wanted to use Kepra's power to create a whole other goddess. She wanted to mold a pupil of her own; Isis knew that she could not make someone a god out of nothing, but she had figured out how to make someone a god, given someone else's essence. No one knew about this, not even Amun himself. All the gods and goddess had wondered why Isis wanted Kepra's essence, but they would never guess what her true intentions had come to be.

No one would ever guess because no one had ever done it before. But Isis was determined that she had the willpower and the advanced magic to do it. She began by mixing some herbs and potions. There was some dark, very dark, magic poured into the cauldron that she was using to mix the ingredients of the potion. Isis added her own blood to the mixture to make the pupils magic without having to go through all the learning phases. She added so many things to make this goddess chaotic and filled with madness.

Last but not least, to make the mixture whole and become a being, she added the goddess essence of Kepra. When she added the essence and finished, the cauldron fizzed and popped with a big explosion that erupted in the cave. Smoke filled the cave, and Isis couldn't see anything but fog. When the smoke dissipated, a beautiful woman stepped out. She had long, straight black hair, with mocha-color skin with natural highlights from the sun. She had bright hazel eyes and a body sculpted from the heavens. Isis's plan had worked; she was delighted to see the new witch. When the new witch got to Isis, she said nothing. She stood in front of her and balled up a fist; when she balled up her fist, everything in the cave that was in glass shattered. She laughed with a high-pitched voice that echoed throughout the whole cave after she was done. The new witch held her palm up, made an instant fireball, and slung it across the cave, lighting up the cave. So much mana was drained from the new witch from using so much with just being born. The new witch dropped to her knees in pain. Isis had already foreseen the new witch using all her stamina quickly. Isis picked the witch up and put her in the bed to rest. Isis looked at the new witch and pushed her hair out of her eyes after placing her on the bed and sitting next to her. Isis stared at the new witch for a second and decided to name her Heka, which meant "the great creative force or life-supporting energy that connects the subjects." Isis was pleased on this day.

Chapter 8
Return Home

In Egypt Kepra was standing up, realizing she wasn't in Orion's belt any longer. She began to stand to her feet and get acclimated to the new environment that she was now calling home. She still had her strength and knowledge but lacked all other key components. Her strength that was there was only slightly depleted by losing her godhood. She was relieved to know she still had her strength, and she was sure she would need it for the journey ahead of her. She was left with the sword that Amun had given her and her fangs of fury. When she had finally gotten herself together, she walked around and examined her surroundings. She began to think of the decision she made and whether it was the right one. She knew she would never see her mother, her friends, or her mentors again. She knew if she reached out to any of them, they would try everything in their power to try to get her to come back, or worse, inform her mother; she knew her mother would make her come home. Kepra then thought she couldn't go home, though... Isis had made sure of that. Kepra didn't want that anyway, though she wanted to be on her own. She wanted to show everyone that she was an adult, old enough to take care of herself and anyone else she deemed fit for her protection. It was her time, and she wasn't going to let anyone try and ruin it for her.

She had missions to complete, and one of them involved finding her rightful mother and father, if there was any truth to the notion or not. She still wanted to look into it. She still wanted to seek answers for herself without having anyone going behind her back lying to her. To Horus and Thoth, who had held a special place in her heart, she would never get to see if there was anything that could truly come from it. She was sad but hopeful for the new adventure that was ahead of her. Kepra grabbed her sword, put it on her back, and decided to walk to a local bar.

Kepra began her journey in a small tavern. She needed time to think and get an understanding of what was happening to her.

Kepra walked in, got a pint in front of the bar, and sat down at a nearby table. While in the tavern, she overheard the conversations of the people of the city. They ranted about a horrible pharaoh who made their wages less and less for the hourly work they did for building the pyramids. On top of the low wages, they also had to pay taxes that were well over the amount they were making to survive. They complained about the soldiers harassing the villagers; everyone was highly upset. It had only been a few seconds of hearing this, and the king's guards slammed the doors open of the tavern. Kepra took a second to evaluate that she no longer had her armor given to her on her birthday but was completely engulfed in womanly attire. The clothes she wore made it slightly difficult to move the normal way she would. With the soldiers making everyone uncomfortable and harassing the villagers, Kepra got up to take a stand for the lot. The soldiers asked Kepra if she didn't want a death wish to sit down and shut up before they gave her what she wanted. Kepra pushed a chair so hard to the front of the tavern that the first two guards in the front fell, and it set the other four in frenzy mode. Kepra lifted her hands and gave the signal to come get some more.

The remaining soldiers flung their swords at Kepra as she managed to block all of them. Soon after, she pulled out the golden blade that Amun had given her. As Kepra was taking the sword from her back, it began to glow. The sword blinded the soldiers, dropping them to their knees with their hands in the air, surrendering. Kepra looked around, and one soldier was trying to escape. She pulled out her fangs and threw them; the swords only tripped the soldier, knocking him on his face to eat dirt. Kepra insisted that the guards give them the money that they gained from the people in the tavern. She told them to leave the villagers alone, or else she would find them. The soldiers got up, shook their heads agreeing, and ran as fast as they could out of the tavern. After the soldiers left, the villagers rejoiced and began to thank Kepra for all she had done for them. They began to drink and celebrate in her honor. But little did Kepra know someone in the crowd was also admiring her from afar, trying to understand who this woman was. Kepra decided to leave soon after the celebration. She continued walking around the city and noticed the guards coming out of the temple of the gods. In their hands, they held the offerings from the villagers who gave to the gods. Kepra approached the soldiers and told them to leave the gods 'offerings alone. The soldiers laughed at the woman in front of them dressed as a mere gypsy threatening their work for today that the pharaoh had given them strict orders to do. She walked to them with nothing but anger in her eyes. There were eight soldiers, and she was determined to get her point across to the pharaoh for such horrible actions. She questioned, stealing from the gods? —will the pharaoh stoop no lower?

One of the soldiers came at her with force, his sword in hand. He lifted it above his head and attacked Kepra running straight for her. Kepra caught the sword with her bare hands and twisted it away from the soldier's hands. Once the sword fell, she kicked him down. The soldier lay there trying to get up. Kepra kneeled, one leg on the ground, and broke his neck. The other soldiers in awe started backing up. Only two more approached Kepra and decided to take her on. She quickly assessed the situation and kicked one in the stomach, dropping him to the ground and then pulling out her sword for the last one. The soldier put all his strength into the fight. Kepra spun the opposite way and punctured the man in the stomach from behind. The soldier whom she had kicked down was now up in front of her. She swept the man from under his feet and then plunged the sword into his body. The other soldiers ran away in defeat and dropped all the offerings for the gods.

Kepra, confused about what sort of man would allow for such betrayal to take place on his watch, was mad. Kepra decided to walk through the market to get something to eat; people slowly started to notice her. She was greeted by a merchant with free bread and fruit; while Kepra was shopping, a person in a dark cloak bumped into her, and Kepra felt something was off. She felt around her body; she noticed she was missing her fangs. She started to run after the cloaked person, only to run into a dead end. The person dropped down from the building and landed right in front of Kepra. Kepra warned the person to give her back her weapon.

The hooded person took out the fangs, examined them, and took the hood from his face. She had no idea who he was. After the young man descended from the building, he questioned Kepra about who she was. Kepra began to tell him she was just a traveler. The young man told her his name was Mentu-her-khepeshef, and his brother had taken his place on the throne when it actually should be him. The man went on to say that he had been watching her in all the fights that she had been having with the soldiers, and to him, it seemed that she was no regular traveler. Then he pulled out the fangs again, looked at them up and down, and said to her, "these look like the gods themselves made them. So, who are you?".

She told them she used to live in Egypt a long time ago and came back to find her parents. The prince thought for a minute and asked when did she leave last? She said she thought it was when she was a baby. Khepeshef looked at her and tried to remember, and he asked Kepra to help him get his throne back to restore order to the kingdom. Kepra agreed, he began to tell her of the sports that were about to happen when the sun rises. He began to tell her the benefit of winning the tourney. They talked for what seemed like forever, and after getting all the information, he insisted on getting some armor before applying to the tournament. She told him she didn't know anyone, nor did she have any money. He told her to go to this secret place where they would graciously open up and give her the armor for free based on all the good things she had been doing around town. He also suggested that she uncover her face, and tear some of the clothes so that she looked different. He didn't want her to draw attention to herself after all the altercations she had been having with the city guards.

After their talk, Kepra walked to the secret place, which the prince gave her instructions to find. When she arrived at the spot, a wooden door looked like it wrapped around for a mile and was painted black. She knocked. There was a peephole, and a gentleman answered the door; she gave them the password the prince said to say. When the door opened, it looked like its own little village inside a village. She wondered how something like this could go unnoticed. The man asked her if she had been here before, and she replied no. He asked her what or who she was looking for; she replied that she was given instructions to find a blacksmith from a man who is the uncrowned prince. The man, embarrassed, told her to hurry and follow him to the man's shop.

Kepra walked with the man and, when approaching the shop, saw all of the beautiful merchandise. Kepra spoke to the blacksmith and told him she was there to obtain armor to fight for the uncrowned prince. He looked at her, nodded his head up and down, and without any words, went to the back of his shop and pulled out Kepra's specific armor. Kepra, confused, asked the man how he came to attain such a gift. The doorman looked at Kepra and told her, "He is mute, my dear.".

Saddened by seeing the armor, with her head low, she thanked the man and started to walk toward the entrance again. Suddenly, she heard loud banging and shouting coming from what seemed like the pharaoh's soldiers. The door man told her to run out the back so that they would not catch her.

In all these years, the soldiers have never found the secret door that led to their black-market village. He told her some-one must have followed her, and she apologized to the door-man. Kepra told him she wasn't going anywhere. He begged her to reconsider based on her armor. If she chose to fight now, they would recognize her when applying to the tourney. He told her the people here would be ok and that they had been praying for someone like her. He told her, "Hurry now, out the back, before someone sees you.".

Kepra ran out the back exit, hopping over people and build-ings, trying to escape. Soon after she got out of harm's way and stopped running. She immediately took off the gypsy clothes and put on her armor. It felt so good to feel it on her body once again. She took a walk in a tavern's direction and retired for the night.

Chapter 9
Gemini

The next morning Kepra woke up, put her armor on, strapped up her boots, and put her weapons on. After she got herself together, she headed out of the tavern and walked to the tournament to sign up. When Kepra got there, she could see that the tournament consisted of combat skills, athletics, and archery. Kepra knew to get an audience with the pharaoh, she had to win this thing; she had to convince everyone, including herself, that she was there to protect the pharaoh and not infiltrate his palace. The winner of the tournament would become the pharaoh's right-hand man/woman and able to ride into battle with him whenever there was war, but better yet, they would earn his trust. She knew that winning at all costs was what she had to do.

The gods looked down from Aaru at the temples that were defiled; they were highly upset with humanity. Amun, furious, decided to take action. Amun went to see Isis about unleashing a power unlike any other to punish humanity for their insolence. Amun knew that Neith's daughter was out there somewhere, but he had to prove a point to the humans acting out. Amun had no clue what Isis truly had in her possession; all he knew is that Isis had the power to create the right amount of chaos to bring back order in the mundane.

Amun arrived in the beyond; he walked into the cave to see Isis mixing up potions and singing. Isis heard Amun approaching them from a mile away before he entered the cave. She hid Heka right before he entered the back of the cave and told her not to move. Amun walked around the cave; he felt like something wasn't right. From the back of the cave, there was a rock that fell. Both Amun and Isis's heads turned to the sound. Isis quickly looked back to Amun and broke the silence from his suspicion with a question: "great Amun, why are you here?".

"Isis," he said, "I know of the betrayal that you have done to our family. I do not know exactly what you have done, but I'm sure it will come to light. For now, I need you to help me bring structure to the mundane. They have acted out for the last time.".

Isis shook her head and agreed with Amun. "Yes, you're right. They have been disobedient, and I will do what must be done, Amun.".

"See that it happens soon, Isis," Amun said as he walked toward the entrance of the cave. She bowed and said, "yes, your greatness." Amun disappeared into the light sky.

Isis walked back in and hurried to the back of the cave to check on Heka. Heka walked out and wondered why she had to be hidden while Amun was there.

Isis took this as an advantage. Isis told Heka that she possessed the godhood of a warrior goddess, and every one of the gods was trying to find her. They did not know yet if they found her, they would not be able to bring her back because Isis had her essence, and without her essence, she could not return. "If they find out you have her essence, they will try to kill you so that it will return to her so that she can come back to Aaru." Isis took Heka by the hand and said to her, "Kepra the warrior goddess and you cannot live in the same universe; you must search all of Egypt and kill her. Only then will you have eternal freedom, and they will never be able to take the essence from you, my child." Heka's eyes squinted; she was filled with vexation.

Heka, who had been learning all she could from Isis, was very powerful at this point; with the goddess soul raging inside her, Heka felt invincible. Heka's power grew with each day. Little did Isis know Heka had plans of her own. Heka had already planned to take over Isis's place, but for now she had to kill the warrior goddess.

Isis was out getting things for Heka's journey to earth; Heka went into Isis's bedroom and looked for Isis's book of shadows. Heka looked everywhere in the large cave. She closed her eyes and envisioned the book. She opened her eyes and scanned the room once again. Her eyes immediately stopped in the closet under the flooring. Heka walked over to the closet and stared at the flooring, and it started to peel up. There was the book; Heka extended her hand, and with one gesture, the book raised and went onto her hand. With the power she already possessed, and now with the most talented witch's spells and enchantments, Heka felt no one could stop her.

Isis got back to the hut to find that Heka had taken off. Isis had a devilish grin on her face. She knew what she had sparked Heka into finding the goddess, and she was pleased with Heka's determination but ignorant to the betrayal of Hekas' thievery.

Heka, not knowing Kepra's exact location, started far away from her. Heka wanted to leave no stone left unturned, and she searched every city and village. Heka burned everything she touched; she was determined to find the warrior woman.

Kepra approached the stand to sign up; after putting her name on the sheet of paper, she began looking around and saw a man who looked as though he competed. The closer she got to him, the more she began to remember this familiar face. It was the man from the market, the day she rendezvoused with Thoth to Egypt. She remembered him specifically because of his beautiful appearance. His hair was brownish orange and of shoulder-length; his skin was olive tan, and it looked like ra himself had kissed it. The young man wore silver armor that caressed every bit of his muscles; he was a magnificent specimen of a human. The armor he wore held the crest of the pharaoh; Kepra wondered what the man was doing competing for his own position. She hoped that he would not recognize her.

People from all over Egypt came to view the tourney; the seats in the arena were filled with Egypt's esteemed people. Kepra was given her selection in the tourney, and she was to be one of the third fighters to compete. All the greatest fighters and athletes were there competing for the position of the first command. Kepra began to get more and more intrigued with the competition; she knew her strength, and her training was much more than any human had seen. Kepra's turn finally arrived, and she had to fight four soldiers who had been in the pharaoh's family army for years. Kepra raised an eyebrow and took a stance. The people observed every moment of the event; she searched around and found where the pharaoh was placed and knew it was time to show off her skill.

One man ran toward her, sword out, ready to throw it into her chest. Kepra pulled her sword out. The gold from the sword sparkled as she took it from its sheath; it caught everybody's eyes. The swords chimed together, and the dance began between her and the men. As she was fighting one of the soldiers, another soldier who was much larger than the others stopped and threw a large spear toward her. The spear was almost to her when she cut and killed the first soldier in front of her. It was just in time to catch the spear midair with one hand. With her sword in her left hand, Kepra hurled the spear into the soldier who had thrown it. The spear spiraled into the large soldier, going straight through his chest. Kepra had only three more soldiers left.

Kepra took out her fangs. She spun her body to a 180 degree and then back in front while releasing the fangs. The fangs hit the wooden pillars in the arena. The soldiers split up and ran toward Kepra, thinking that that weapon had no clear direction. While she was fighting the two soldiers, she cut one and beheaded the other while the other soldier approached her back side and thought he finally had the best of her. The fangs came back and cut him right through the middle, cutting him in half. Kepra then caught the fangs in her hand and put them back on her side.

The crowd went wild, wanting more from the warrior Kepra. The soldiers heard the crowd. With eyes on the pharaoh, they released a bear and a boar with sharp tusks based on the pharaoh's instructions. Kepra leaped at the bear with a sword in hand. She landed just before the bear; the bear ran toward her with a mighty stride. Kepra ran toward the bear; just before Kepra got to the bear, she slid underneath the bear with sword out and cut him from neck to tail. With Kepra bloody and looking for the boars, she ran over to the sides of the area where random weapons were hanging up. She scanned the weapons for a bow. She finally saw it and ran toward it. Next to the bow were arrows below in a pot. She took the bow and one of the arrows. She lit the arrow on fire with one of the lights that surrounded the arena's gates. The arrow that was lit on fire was shot into the eye of the boar.

Once the boar was struck, it started to roll around, scrambling for relief. Kepra quickly ran to the boar, dropping the bow. She then pulled out her sword and twisted it in her hand, coming down on the boar and taking its life. The crowd went crazy, and the pharaoh could not deny the strength of this woman. He was in awe already. Kepra knew with a performance like that, there was no doubt she was being looked at to fill the role.

The games came to an end for the day and were to reconvene at ra's first awakening. The pharaoh came to the barracks where the athletes were currently training for the next day. The pharaoh was so amazed at the woman that he asked her to come back to the palace and dine with him to talk about being a part of his army.

Meanwhile in Alexandria, Heka was destroying not only the people but also hope and faith. Heka was seducing the men and killing the women and children. Those she did not kill vowed their allegiance to her. They began to worship her and shunned all the other gods. She would then snatch their souls from their body, making them the living dead. She went from city to city doing this, creating a mighty army. She was coming for Kepra, and when she did, all of Egypt would also be hers.

Kepra joined the pharaoh at his palace; the pharaoh had his cooks prepare a feast that would have made the ancestors jealous. Kepra and the pharaoh talked, and he explained what he wanted to do as far as conquering the surrounding countries. He needed every cent in Egypt so that he could create an army no one had ever seen. Kepra hated being around the pharaoh, knowing all the nonsense acts he committed. The people of Egypt had trusted him to lead them into prosperity and favorability with the gods. Instead, they got a tyrant who thought of nothing but conquering. Kepra and the pharaoh continued to go over what he saw Egypt becoming over the next couple of years. The pharaoh looked down for a second to grab a bite to eat when all of a sudden, he saw an arrow spiraling in his direction, coming straight for his head.

Chapter 10
A Mother Knows

The pharaoh, in shock, without a second to think or could react, closed his eyes in fear of death. A fanglike weapon disposed of the arrow right before it could pierce the pharaoh. Kepra had saved the pharaoh. The pharaoh peeked opened his eyes, in disbelief that he was still alive. He looked around and then on the ground, his eyes had a sense of relief in them after seeing the arrow on the ground. The pharaoh asked what happened. The guards held the misfit guilty of the attack pinned up and ready to take him to the dungeon. One of the guards looked at Kepra and pointed saying, "she saved you, your highness.".

The other guard said, "we found this man hiding; this is the man who threw the arrow, your grace." The pharaoh walked over to his attacker; he wore all black and covered himself in an all-black hood. The pharaoh spit on him as he got closer. He looked at him in the eyes and told him, "You cannot kill a god; guards, take him away.".

He looked at Kepra and thanked her for saving his life. "You will be most rewarded. Kepra, name your price.".

"I wish for nothing, your grace," she said.

He said, "really?".

"Yes," Kepra said. Kepra knew she could not let the old pharaoh die just yet. She had to put someone on the throne she thought would best suit it. She had to make sure the throne went to Khepeshef. Kepra knew her saving the pharaoh's life ensured his trust in her.

After all the commotion had stopped, and everyone was safe, his parents joined the pharaoh and Kepra. They stood as the two entered. He introduced them to Nefertari and Ramesses the ii. They sat down and continued eating. Everyone was talking and getting acquainted. Kepra asked how long the pharaoh's parents had reigned before the new pharaoh took the throne. Nefertari answered, "such a long time ago." Kepra was curious about what she had talked about with the uncrowned prince.

Kepra then asked if there was anyone back in that time who had given a baby to the gods to succeed in a war. The former king and queen looked at each other a second and then looked at her and declined the notion.

With the pharaoh being so self-centered, he failed to give his parents Kepra's name; he kept referring her to as "the great-est warrior" or "best warrior." The parents did not know the entire time they were talking to their daughter. After the din-ner was over, the pharaoh showed Kepra the palace and where she would command her troops once she won. The pharaoh had great faith in her winning the tourney. "You know I've already put in my mind you will be my next in command," the pharaoh said.

Kepra chuckled. "Is that so, your grace? What makes you so sure of that?" She questioned.

"Your skill. I've never seen anything like it; where did you learn to fight as you do?".

She scratched the back of her head and said, "um, I guess I'm just self-taught. Long nights and early mornings.".

"Ahh, yes, I can imagine. Well, nonetheless I insist on you are staying here tonight. It's the least I can do for you saving my life. You're going to need a good night's sleep for tomor-row. I need you well rested.".

Kepra agreed to the nice gesture. The pharaoh clapped his hands and had one of the servants that was nearby put clothes in a guest room and run a hot bath. The servant said, "yes, your grace," and hurried off.

The pharaoh walked the warrior to the dining hall where they first started off and saw that one of the other servants showed Kepra to her quarters. "I will see you in the morning, Kepra. Sleep well." She thanked the pharaoh for the hospitality and followed the servant. The servant walked Kepra to her room and told her there would be clothes to change into in the dresser and hot water in the tub to bathe. She thanked the servant, and the servant went on their way.

Kepra got into her room. She peered into the dresser and took out a nightgown and placed it on the bed. Next, Kepra headed into the bathroom, where there was a hot, steamy bath awaiting her. She slowly walked in the tub. It was deep. There were rose petals on top of the water, which smelled of jasmine, and there were candles lit around it. Kepra completely submerged herself in the water, she took a deep breath, and let out a silent sigh. She was finally relaxed. It felt great, if only for a second. It was quiet in the room—almost too quiet.

Kepra overheard a sound from outside the door. She heard someone walk past her door, and she began to get out of the bath to reach for her sword. Kepra was never far from it. Kepra, naked and dripping with water, held her sword in her hand; she was right by the door hinge. She knew someone was about to open the door, and she was ready. The door opened, and it was Nefertari. Kepra relaxed and caught herself from attacking.

Nefertari gasped; Kepra apologized for frightening her. Kepra headed over to the bed to put the nightgown on. As she was getting dressed, the former queen began to ask her who she was, and Kepra said that she was merely a traveler passing by who wanted to better her life. Nefertari asked how did you know there was a baby given to the gods.

Kepra said she just heard the tale a long time ago, something her mother told her when she was little. Nefertari said she thought she might have been that baby. Nefertari went on to say she was that woman, the woman who gave her pride and joy away; she said as she cried, "her name was Kepra, and I gave her to the gods to help our county.".

Nefertari started crying and sobbing louder, explaining to the great warrior that she never meant to give her baby away. Nefertari went on to say that now she was stuck with her youngest son ruling, who was destroying Egypt brick by brick. Nefertari continued rambling. "I had so much to teach her and tell her, like—".

And before Nefertari could get out another word, a guard knocked on the door to ask Kepra if she was all right. The queen quickly hushed; she didn't want anyone to know she was there. The former queen had been in the palace for so long she knew the ins and outs of the palace.

There was a secret door within the room that the queen used and asked her not to say anything about their conversation tonight as she left the room. Nefertari knew if her son the pharaoh found out about the child that was given away was actually hers all along, he would search everywhere to make sure she could not take his throne. The guard knocked and came into the room and asked the warrior if she was sure. He said he thought he heard someone else's voice and that she didn't respond, so he decided to check on her. After Kepra had confirmed that she was ok, the guard left. Kepra had found her real mother. She was so happy but so sad. Her mother had been dealing with so much internally because she gave her away. Kepra was hurt that she gave her up, but she understood. She loved her mother no less for trying to do what was best for her country. She knew that it must have been a hard sacrifice for her. Kepra finally found what she was looking for, for so long. She had found her parents, only to find the man who was ruling was her brother, which meant that Khepeshef also had to be. She needed to talk to the prince once again to get the full story. He remembered her as a baby; he was the oldest. How did this pharaoh take his place?

The next morning the tourney continued; it was getting down to its last competitors. Kepra and the pharaoh were escorted to the arena. When Kepra arrived, she found out shortly after that she was to battle the attractive man she had seen in the market a while back. Kepra didn't like it; she didn't want to hurt the man, and all of the battles were to the death. The man enticed her; something about him had Kepra on edge when she was around him. Kepra had to make up a plan, and she had to hurry. They were the first to fight. The pharaoh wanted his best warriors to set the tourney off right. Kepra checked her weapons and made sure her armor was intact while heading to one side of the gates that entered the arena. The gates raised, releasing the warriors opposite from each other. They both came out of the enclosed gates. The man twirled his sword in his hand and pulled his shield closer to his body as he inched farther and farther toward Kepra. He looked in her eyes, and she his. The ray from ra hit the man's face, and she could see his eyes clearer. They were of a hazel color with a hint of green. Now that she was in front of him, she could examine all of him from head to toe. The man had a short beard that cuffed his jawline and led to his mustache, which outlined his thick lips.

Kepra began to get into position, ready to fight, but she could not shake the dreamlike state the man had around him for some reason. The handsome man rushed at Kepra and swung his sword at her. Before he could land a hit, Kepra senses sparked, and she quickly blocked his attack. Both of the swords collided; if the man's sword went up, so did Kepra's.

Kepra could do this all day, but she knew the man couldn't. He was good; his fighting techniques were amazing. This only made Kepra more fond of him. They fought for hours; Kepra feared that the pharaoh would not let them go so easily. Kepra, still not wanting to harm the man, flipped her sword in her hand and faked like she was going to strike him in the chest, and then dropped to the ground, sweeping the man from up under his feet. She then quickly put the sword to his neck so that he would not get up nor attack. Kepra shouted out to the pharaoh, "I cannot kill this man for you, great pharaoh; he is a magnificent fighter. I believe you still owe me one request from last night. My request is made here and now. Allow him to live and ride next to me in battle, protecting our city within your army.".

The pharaoh stood up sighed and shook his head, agreeing to her request. The pharaoh motioned for the gates to go up for the two to pass. Kepra helped the man up to his feet. It had been the first battle in history within the arena where one person did not die. After the man got up, they shook in arms, and he thanked her. The handsome man and Kepra left the field and headed back into the barracks. The handsome man came around to Kepra's side of the barracks where she was sitting. She could see him walking from her peripheral. Kepra was sharpening her sword. The man stopped about halfway to her before he asked, "why did you wait all that time to put me on my back? I'm sure you could have been killed me.".

Kepra responded with, "I didn't want to kill you, and by me not wanting to kill you, I had to come up with the idea that the pharaoh could not refuse. I wasn't lying when I said you're great in combat, though.".

"Coming from you, I guess that's a compliment," he said as he chuckled a little. He stared at her for a second and then squinted his eyes. Kepra could tell he was trying to remember her face. "Hey, you know, you look a bit familiar, you know that? Have we met before?" He asked.

She looked to put her head down to seem as if she were studying her sword so that he could no longer see her face and said, "nope. Never seen you a day in my life. Maybe I just have one of those familiar faces.".

"Well, nonetheless, I wanted to thank you for saving me. What's your name?" He asked. "My name is Kepra. Yours?".

"My name is Ankh. I am the head of the military, or so I was.".

"What happened?" She asked.

"I was against doing all the looting from the temples and our people. The pharaoh was going to kill me, but his father overruled it. So, I am nothing more than a wanderer. I joined the tourney to try and regain my rank. I don't know what you did for the pharaoh, but it must have been grave. He would have been more than pleased with my demise.".

"I saved his life, and to add to things, he wants me to take over leading his army. So, he owed the hell out of me. I do commend you for taking a stand on your own and going against the pharaoh; that was very brave.".

"Yeah, well, look where it got me." He laughed. "Kepra, it was nice meeting you. I'm going to go get ready to head out; I'll see you around.".

"You better. You're my next in command!" She yelled out as he was walking away.

The next day, Kepra went back into the arena. It was the last event; Kepra had to fight the last of the best. It was an arena war. All of the soldiers who were left from fighting the last couple of days would be in the arena at one time. The last person standing would win the tourney. Kepra was behind one of the gates waiting to be released. She ran in place and moved her shoulders clockwise to prepare her body for what she was about to endure. The gates finally opened slowly, and the crowd went wild. Kepra could see that the arena had changed. There were huge boulders in the middle, and fire was surrounding them.

Not long after the gates were up, the warriors went into a frenzied state. Kepra pulled her sword out as a fighter ran toward her. She rushed one with a jump kick and then flipped backward, just in time to slash another straight through the neck as she landed on her feet behind him. There were four men; two were down. She singled out the last two and began to fight with them. The two men came at her, one from the back and one from the front. Right before the soldiers got to her, she jumped up in the air, flipping in front of the man who was in front, allowing the soldier from the back to slash completely into the man in front. Kepra then turned to the man behind her, pulled out her dagger from her boot, and threw it in his head. Walking to the man with the dagger in his head, she turned it, twisting it into his skull. After she was certain he was dead, she then took it out placing it back into her boot.

Kepra had defeated all the competitors. She had won. The crowd roared in excitement, screaming, "we want more! we want more! we want more!".

The pharaoh signaled the guard to release one more contestant.

Chapter 11
Moment of Truth

The finale came, and only one man was standing between her and victory. Kepra was annoyed; she should have guessed the pharaoh had more in store for the tournament. She heard the gates opening; she turned in the direction of the gate only to see a hideous man who wore the helmet of a bull, bulky and hideous, with scars and black paint all over his body. He put the helmet on and let out a mighty roar while beating his chest. He bent over and ran toward Kepra at lightning speed. The ruthless man was getting closer. Kepra assessed the situation in a matter of seconds and knew what she had to do. First, she knew she needed to stay far away from the helmet. The helmet itself had two pointy horns.

Just before the bull-man got to Kepra, he stood up and took out his sword. He threw his sword at her. She struck it away with one hit, but by that time, the bull-man was right in front of her and scratched the side of her stomach. He ran right through her to the other side, waiting for her to see the wound so he could head back and strike again. Kepra looked down at the blood dripping from her and put her hand there. She had never seen her blood before; immortals could not die from a human blade nor be punctured. A god would immediately heal if the weapon were not made from Ptah himself. She wiped the blood with her hand and stared at it for a moment. The bull and said aloud, "there is more where that came from, girl.".

Kepra was angry. She turned around, letting out a yell, running towards the bull-man tearing through his defense. As Kepra was fighting the bull, she got a closer look at the helmet. This was not an ordinary helmet; the gods had made it. As she was fighting him, she could see the hieroglyphics that stood for Isis. Kepra ran to the middle of the arena and front-flipped onto the tallest boulder with her sword steadied on the bull-man. The bull-man walked over to the middle of the arena and asked, "why are you running, girl? Let's get this over with.".

Kepra yelled down at him, "I will continue only when you have told me where you got that helmet.".

"I received this gift from the beautiful Isis herself; she sent her regards and told me not to let you walk out of this arena alive," he said as he spit on the dirt.

Kepra let out a warrior's cry and flipped off the boulder, landing just behind the bull-man. She was convinced now that Isis had it out for her. Kepra struck at the bull's helmet, and it flew off. The bull turned around and lunged at Kepra with his sword. Their swords collided; all that you could hear was rattling from the two weapons. Kepra and the villain were fighting hard, swords rattling. Kepra jumped back to avoid a blow, and she fell on her back from being pushed back into a stone. Kepra knew she had to move fast; with a quick release from her lips of "mother, help me," she felt an overwhelming, radiant love come over her, and she regained all strength. She kicked the bull-looking man in the kneecaps while getting up. He fell immediately. Gathering his strength, he got up and slung his sword at her. She moved swiftly out of the way and took out her fangs without throwing them. She pulled them apart and fought with them. She emptied her mind and focused her energy on the dual blades. The blades could feel her connecting with them and began to pulse with a poisonous green. The bull could feel her strength. It was like none other he had ever encountered.

He ran to the helmet and put it back on, but it was too late. Kepra was right behind him. With every blow from Kepra, the bull died a little more. The last blow was delivered to the neck, where she slit it, dropping the bull's body. The helmet rolled off with the head as his lifeless body dropped. Kepra severed the head then grabbed the man's head and threw it in front of the pharaoh. Kepra looked at the crowd, and they went insane. Kepra looked back to reclaim the helmet, but there was only black soot. The helmet had disintegrated with the death of its owner. This was it; the finale was over.

At last, Kepra was the victor. The pharaoh got up and calmed the crowd. He announced that she was the winner. "Kepra, the warrior sent from the gods, is your new commander in chief. You will respect her as if she is me when you see her. Thank you for coming to the games, now it it's time to celebrate.".

When the pharaoh announced her name to the crowds, the former king's and queen's mouths dropped; they were speechless. They didn't want to alarm anyone, so they remained calm and decided to keep it to themselves until later. In the far-off distance, another concerned parent finally knew of the whereabouts of her lost child. The prayer that Kepra had sent out to give her strength was to her mother goddess of war.

Shortly after the battle, the pharaoh came to Kepra and congratulated her on her success and said they would forever tell stories of the warrior goddess of Egypt. As the celebration went on throughout the city, the pharaoh and the former pharaohs and Kepra were escorted to the palace by the guards. When they approached the palace gates, Kepra asked the pharaoh if she could take a night stroll within the city; the king graciously gave permission and told her to be in his presence at first sight of a moving sun. She agreed, hopped off the chariot, and walked into the night. Nefertari was concerned and eager to talk to her child but knew she had to wait a little while longer. Kepra fixated on the night sky, looked up, felt the warm sensation she had felt on the battlefield earlier that day, and all of a sudden, she saw a bright light approach her. It was like a shooting star that touched the earth, and it was her mother.

Neith was so happy to see her; she immediately hugged her and was crying profusely. "I have been so worried about you," Neith said. "You left and didn't tell anyone where you were going, and I told you not to come here—".

Before she finished talking, Kepra said, "you lied to me; my whole life has been a lie. I had to rely on the wisdom of a witch that I did not even trust to give me information that I was seeking my whole life from you.".

Neith, in disbelief, shook her head and said Kepra, "I was going to tell you, I really was, but you are my child; you being from this place makes no difference.".

"don't you get it? You took me from my family. I was nothing more than a sacrifice to save my people. You hurt a family that did nothing but worship the ground you walked on, and you did that to repay them," Kepra said, frustrated.

"Kepra, you don't understand. I did it because Amun commanded me to. He told me I had to make war so great that the pharaohs had no choice but to feel that the only thing worthy enough to give was you. He asked me to train you and love you, and I did. I have had nothing but love for you ever since the day I first saw you, Kepra; you have to believe me. I love you; you are from me because I raised you," Neith cried.

Kepra walked off from her mom. While walking off, Kepra said, "you want someone to forgive you? Forgive yourself first, mother." With that being said, Kepra ran off in the distance. Kepra knew that she could not ultimately run from her mother, knowing that she knew where she was now. Kepra needed silence at the moment, and she had to get away; there were too many emotions built up erupting. Kepra felt such anger for her mother still; she couldn't believe she would hold back all of this from her. Kepra let out a sigh of relief; even though she was angry, it.

Felt good actually to know the whole truth. It felt good actually to have the conversation with her mother. Kepra felt she could try and heal now.

All this was running through Kepra's head as she moved through the city until she couldn't run any farther. She had bent over to catch her breath right before approaching the waterfall that was by the red sea and the Mediterranean. There was lush greenery everywhere. For a second, it felt like she wasn't in Egypt anymore. She walked, climbed up to the top, and threw rocks into the sea, still trying to calm down and think rationally.

Neith tried to approach Kepra again. Neith came out of the darkness and walked on the water to her daughter. Neith said, "my love, I have brought your pet to protect you. I realize you are angry with me, but there is something that is of great concern. I am relieved you called on me when you did actually. You gave Isis your godhood, correct?" Neith asked Kepra.

Kepra agreed.

"I hate to tell you this, and I will be by your side all the way...".

"Mother, spit it out; what's wrong?" Kepra screamed.

"Isis has released a benevolent witch that is starting to consume all of Egypt. She is very powerful and holds Isis's spell book. Who knows? Rumors have it she might even surpass Isis at this point," Neith said with sorrow.

"Ok, and so what does that have to do with me?" Kepra asked.

Neith stopped for a minute to regain her thoughts. "Kepra, Isis took your essence to make this new god; that was her intention the whole time. It was never to help you in any way; she wanted your godhood to leave you helpless and to erase you from existence. The new god, Heka, is the one who holds the key to you regaining your godhood. The worst part of it all is that she knows that. Isis has put it into her head that to keep her life. She must see to it that you never retrieve your essence.".

Kepra shook her head softly back and forth. "I can't believe this, and I should have known there was a price to pay." Kepra looked at her mother's worried face and said, "mother, don't worry. I will figure this out; I have the strategies of the greatest warriors known to man and the knowledge of the best scholar. I will succeed. You have no reason to worry." There was a brief pause in the conversation, and then Kepra began talking again.

"The people here seem like they are losing hope in the gods and are asking why you guys are not helping them.".

"Kepra, Amun did what he thought would be best; he had to scare the humans for them to respect us again. Aaru sakes, Kepra, they were pillaging and plundering our temples for offerings, but Amun regretted his decision. He did not know that Isis had this planned. Isis can't even control her anymore. I don't know what we're going to do about her, but something must be done; she must be stopped," Neith said.

"you're right; I will put an end to this abomination," Kepra said.

"But Kepra, you are human now; what can you do against her?" Neith proclaimed. "Mother, I am still the warrior that you taught, and some of my strength remains. Trust me, please.".

Neith quietly nodded. All of a sudden, Neith overheard something in the distance rattling through the leaves. Aten roared and went to find what it is. The uncrowned prince walked out and said, "call your beast off. Please, I'm sorry for following you." Khepeshef came closer, and Neith disappeared quickly while blowing a kiss at her daughter. Khepeshef said,

"I knew you were different; I just couldn't figure out what it was about you.".

Kepra said, "what all did you hear?".

He said, "everything. Your parents are here in this world, but you were raised with the gods?".

She nodded and said yes.

He continued, "then... Your parents must be mine?".

She looked off into the waterfall and said, "yes, I am your sister, and I am no longer a god. I came down to search for our parents and to cure the ache that I have to be a part of this world, your world." He just sat there for a minute staring off. He had no words for her.

Khepeshef then remembered why he had come to talk to her. He then said to her, "well, you have won the competition. I hear you are the warrior goddess of Egypt now, a great name. You do realize that it is only a matter of time before father and mother figure out who you are, don't you?".

She said, "I think they know already; they announced my name at the tourney. Not looking forward to having a heart to heart with them about it.".

He was mad at her answer. He didn't understand. Still, she told him they could have given the gods anything, and they chose her. She thought, did they care nothing for my life? He said, "they loved their people. You of all the gods should understand because you have been doing it since you arrived here.".

As he tried to comfort her, they sat and made up a plan on how they would take out the pharaoh. After the plan was complete, Khepeshef took off with the words of "I'll see you soon, sister," on his lips. Kepra was stunned at the words that he uttered but knew nothing was far from the truth. She had two brothers: one who made life a living hell for the people of Egypt and the other, who wanted nothing more than peace. Kepra had two missions to fulfill: one to place the rightful pharaoh on the throne and the other to slay Heka. Kepra went into deep thought as Aten got closer to console her. She had huge responsibilities on her hands, and she wasn't going to stop until they were complete.

Chapter 12
Knowing Is Half the Battle

Kepra could see the sun was on the horizon, so she hurried and hopped on Aten's back to return to the palace. Kepra left Aten outside the gates of the palace and hid him. No explanation could be given if he was detected. Kepra ran into the palace to her room, and Kepra quickly bathed and met with the pharaoh. Kepra had told Aten not to draw attention unless she called on him. He roared to agreed and stayed in earshot near the woods waiting for Kepra's call. Kepra showed her face, and the pharaoh told her that there was a great disturbance in Egypt from a witch that claimed she is more powerful than the gods. Kepra was not alarmed at him telling her this, for she had already discovered information on the witch.

"She is starting her army, and they are half dead; I've heard. It looks like the underworld has formed on earth," the pharaoh said. The pharaoh and Kepra decided on a plan for the army to annihilate the witch Heka. They brought the troops together to start their training. Ankh was among them; he was to be her second in command. After a long day of training, preparing the army for the war ahead, Kepra decided to retire for the night. Kepra headed back to her room; once inside, she could feel someone watching her. Kepra was human now; she could no longer see the gods unless they wanted her to. Horus revealed himself to her; he grabbed her and hugged her. She had missed this love, his love. Horus took Kepra's face in his hand and moved her face closer to his. He paused midway from her lips and then took her breath away with a kiss. The kiss was deep and longed for.

She pulled back halfway, stared at him in his eyes for a second, and then kissed him again. They lost control of themselves due to the passion between them. Horus missed her; he missed her body, her smell, everything. Horus told Kepra to close her eyes, so she did. He took her somewhere on the planet that looked so beautiful; the heavens would be jealous. She opened her eyes and asked, "where have you taken me, Horus?" She laughed as she examined the surreal place surrounding them. It had clear blue water, and the sun was just about to set in the pink, blue, and orange sky. There was a cabana on the shore of a white-sand beach.

"I didn't want anyone to hear you scream; you know I don't like being quiet." He chuckled, trying to get a rise out of Kepra with his scandalous words.

"Great Horus, if I didn't know any better, I would think you are trying to bed me, a mere human warrior," Kepra said as she ran into his arms. They were covered in sand from play fighting around. After they were done, Horus picked Kepra up and led her to the bed. The night escaped Kepra; she awoke in her bed at the palace. Horus was waiting for her to come to; he was right by her bedside when she awoke. Kepra rubbed her eyes to focus them from the sunlight that was coming into the room. When she turned to her right Horus was next to her; she was thrilled that he did not leave.

"I wanted to stay and talk to you about everything that was going on; Neith told everyone about my mother's malicious plan." Horus leaned into Kepra and grabbed her face. "I'm so sorry that she is doing this to you; I will not rest until I know you are safe from her, my love," he said.

Kepra smiled; she knew Horus loved her more than anything. "You know why she wants me dead, right?" Kepra asked him. He shrugged his shoulders in confusion. "You!" She raised her voice while giggling a little. "She wants you to be with Hathor. She has always thought that I'm not good enough for you; she hated seeing us together, Horus.

"I've caused all this drama just by wanting to find my parents. I could have avoided all this. If it weren't for me, there would be no Heka, no—".

"Kepra, stop feeling sorry for yourself; human or not, you're still the best damn warrior on this planet. Kepra, did you know all of us individually had to go through our challenges to be the gods we are today? Trust me; you're just in a trial-god phase; things will work out.".

"Annnnd what if they don't?".

"Kepra, all you do is have to defeat Heka. You will be a god again. Your essence will be restored unto you.".

She said, "it sounds good and all, but she's stronger than me.".

Horus looked at her with disbelief and said, "really? Because last time I checked, your mother, Thoth, and I gave you the best combat training and knowledge a god could ever come across. Plus, your armor and weaponry are made from the great Ptah himself. You should not doubt your skills. The sword you have—I bet you still have not acquired its full potential. Have faith in yourself, Kepra, and you can do the unthinkable," he said as he kissed her on the forehead.

There was a knock on the door. Horus left after Kepra's attention was averted towards the door. "Warrior Kepra, the men are ready for your training." One of the soldiers yelled out. Kepra grabbed her stuff and headed out into the barracks. She trained for a few hours; she gave the army strict orders about fighting against the enemy. They were doing great; she was proud of them. A couple more days of intense training, and they should be ready, she thought to herself.

After training, the men were hungry. She followed them to the cafeteria to eat. She wanted to show the men that they were a unit in everything they did. Gaining their trust was everything to her. She was there for them, and they respected her for it. She would die in battle next to them if it came down to it. After Kepra grabbed some gruel, she sat at a table by herself. Ankh saw her while he was in line waiting for food. He joined her. He started talking about the war to come; she stopped the conversation. "Hey, Ankh, how many kids did the former pharaohs have?".

"Shh." He hushed her and said to her. "We don't talk about that here; the pharaoh doesn't like anyone bringing up how many siblings he has due to an event that led him to inherit the throne. He thinks no one knows if no one talks about it," he said as he rolled his eyes. He asked her to walk to the local tavern; little did he know it was where she first started her journey in Egypt.

They finished eating and started to walk out of the barracks, not realizing they had caught the eye of a curious soldier. They walked into the tavern, and the innkeeper immediately recognized Kepra; he told her drinks were on the house. Ankh wondered what she could have possibly done to make the innkeeper and the villagers in the tavern so happy to see her. "Jeez, you're like a god to them; what did you do?".

"Ahh, nothing, just helped out a few friends," Kepra replied.

The soldier following them stole a hooded cape from the wall when walking in to disguise himself. While walking in after them, he immediately noticed that the last time he was here was because of a woman of similar strength. While in the tavern, the soldier overheard the innkeeper talking to the warrior and was curious about the occasion for such a celebration. He walked through the crowd and got a seat right behind the warrior so that he could hear everything. Still in disguise, he tugged at the hood to cover his face more, making sure no one would recognize him.

Kepra began to talk about how she had come to the village looking for her parents and ran across a prince that was to hear him tell it, the rightful pharaoh. Ankh looked shocked and, without thinking, said, "I know him, just never told anyone because the king doesn't want anyone snooping around trying to figure out the truth, I suppose. Talking about this around anyone and it getting back to the pharaoh is a penalty by death.".

Ankh said he felt like things had changed; the land was so happy and prosperous until this pharaoh took reign. "They say Khepeshef had been well groomed to become the next pharaoh of the two brothers, not the one we have now.".

Kepra asked, "what happened?".

Ankh told her all he remembered was this: "one day before the coronation for Khepeshef, he overheard fighting from the two princes' room and decided to listen in from the closed door. The pharaoh in leadership now threatened the prince with killing their parents in their sleep.".

Kepra gasped and held her hand over her mouth and questioned, "who would do such a thing?".

Ankh went on, "that day, the prince made a very hard decision, though heartbreaking. While leaving his people in the hands of a madman, he knew what he had to do. He agreed to the king and, during the coronation, gave the crown to his brother. No one knew the exact reason for the travesty. Still, the people had no choice to go along with it and bowed to their new ruler.".

Kepra asked, "does anyone else know about this?".

"no. No one even knows that I know.".

Kepra began to feel like she could trust Ankh and told him of who she was and the real reason they were so ecstatic to see her here in the tavern. The soldier had gotten all that he wanted and more; he slowly exited the tavern and made his way back to the palace to tell the pharaoh. As the warrior and

Ankh were leaving the tavern, a feeling of caution came over her, and she told him as they were walking back. When they approached the palace gates, the soldier immediately tried to arrest them. Kepra called out, "where is the pharaoh? Let me see him.".

The pharaoh approached the other soldiers, he pushed by them, getting to the front of the line to see Kepra. "So, you are the pest that I was hunting all along, that was targeting my men. You tried to stop me from collecting my taxes and my offerings. Ahh, and Ankh, not a surprise to see you helping someone try and take me down. Maybe this was all your plan to begin with," the pharaoh said.

Kepra and Ankh were now surrounded with the guards and the pharaoh; they were coming in closer the more the pharaoh spoke. "a little birdie tells me the real reason you have come to my country. Kepra, goddess of war... Or should I say, warrior of war"—the pharaoh laughed maniacally while trying to make fun of Kepra no longer being a goddess— "you have committed treason. Kepra and Ankh and will be beheaded for such.".

He then looked at Ankh and said, "I never knew anyone knew the story of my brother and me, not even our parents knew, but that will all be over when they behead the two of you," he said. The pharaoh laughed. "The irony of me calling you the warrior sent from the true gods. I hope they save you from your death and see you into Aaru." The pharaoh left and walked back into the palace. While walking back, he said, "capture them, and if they don't make it to the executioner, so be it.".

The guards had formed a circle around Ankh and Kepra; they were closing in on them. Kepra hurried and called out for Aten. Aten came with lightning speed; she had never seen him fly so fast. He demolished the warriors to bits in pieces; Kepra hopped on his back and grabbed Ankh and lifted him on as well. Aten ran as far as he could then defended into the sky.

Not long after, they were in the woods by the waterfall with the pyramids in the distance. It was beautiful and relaxing. Kepra needed this time to think. Kepra sat on a rock not that far from the waterfall, and Ankh came and sat next to her. Aten was lying near a tree fast asleep. Ankh thanked her for saving him, but he could see she was sad. He asked her if she was all right; she apologized for getting him in trouble. She only wanted to know how this terrible man could be in power. He told her not to worry. He hated the pharaoh. He only worked for him because his mother and her mother had also worked for the previous kings and queens. It was sort of like a family tradition.

She looked at the waterfall, trying to clear her mind; she stood up from Ankh and asked him to join her for a swim. He asked what she was talking about. Kepra started to disrobe. As she took her clothes off, he looked, watching her body glisten from moonlight, hitting her beautiful curves. After being completely undressed, she quickly jumped in the water and headed to the waterfall. Ankh looked at her body; her skin complexion radiated with colors of the sun and the sand in the desert. He decided to jump into the water; he undressed. First the breastplate and then the bottom. She stared; she had been fascinated with him since she saw him in the market that day. His skin was a dark brown with a hint of golden undertones, his hair had hints of red pigmentations. His hair had tight curls. His muscles were chiseled like the statutes that mortal depicted of the gods. His physique was impeccable; he dived into the water. It was at least ten feet deep. It was warm like bathwater; he approached her. They stood side by side for a moment letting the water from the waterfall fall on their bodies. Ankh got closer to her and ran his fingers through her hair. With his other hand, he touched her shoulder and ran that hand down her arm, grabbing her hand and intertwining it with his. He pulled her in close to him and kissed her. That night they explored every part of each other's bodies and slept alongside the bay of the sea.

The next morning, they decide to find Khepeshef and get a new plan together. They figured that with Ankh's knowledge of the palace and Kepra's techniques, they could surely get to the pharaoh. He would either give the crown over easily, or he would die for it. Either way, he was giving up his position. The mere fact of this crazy man being around her parents drove her insane, and the idea of him trying to kill them was ludicrous, all to take the throne. He had to pay for his actions, and she would make sure he did. Ankh and Kepra walked through the village all day to try and find Khepeshef, but there was no sign of him. It was getting late in the day, and finally, they found him near the secret wall she had ventured into to get her armor, dressed in black from head to toe so no one would suspect who he was. Once they got closer, he quickly turned around and became defensive; as soon as he saw who it was, his guard was lowered. He asked Kepra what she was doing there and why she would bring this man who had given the oath to serve the pharaoh. She told him what happened to them at dusk of yesterday. He held his head and said, "what do we do now, princess?".

After she heard this, her face swiftly changed from problem-solving to being insulted. She knew now who she was, but that did not necessarily mean that she wanted to reclaim that title. She was content with just being the warrior of Egypt. Kepra told Khepeshef about a plan she had been thinking of while trying to locate him that day. When the prince heard the plan, he agreed that it was a formidable one, and later that night, they followed through with it. Kepra, Ankh, and the prince, all in black robes with armor underneath, advanced to the palace. They were there to bring about justice. Ankh showed the map that he had made before they got there of the palace. He showed Kepra and Khepeshef the pharaoh's bedroom and showed them the locations of every guard who was on duty and their posts that they were defending at that time.

Kepra knew she had to be stealthy, but she also knew she had to let her brother do most of the work. He was the one who had been tormented all of his life due to this imposter. There were a couple of guards they had to cross paths with, but it was nothing that Kepra couldn't handle. She had seen all their skills and knew they lacked many things to make them great; she would use this to her advantage. As they got closer to the soldiers, Kepra hid and then sneaked behind them, snapping some of their necks and slashing some of their voice boxes so as not to make a noise. As they started to reach the bedroom, the queen was in his bedroom, and she stood there watching him sleep. Kepra was startled and not prepared for her; she thought quickly and improvised.

The two went into the bedroom and sneaked up on their mother. Khepeshef put one hand over her mouth so that she wouldn't scream. She was frightened but quickly realized it was her and Khepeshef and asked why they were there. Kepra said, "there is no time for this; the guards will be alerted any minute now. Do what you must," she whispered to her little brother.

He looked at her and nodded his head and then drew his sword. The queen yelled out, "no!".

The pharaoh's eyes rose, but it was too late; Khepeshef had already penetrated his body with the sword. He bled out, but before he died, "well done, brother" left his lips.

The queen hollered out, alerting all of the guards who were in attendance. Khepeshef took off his disguise. The guards instantaneously bowed to the new pharaoh; with a sigh of relief, Kepra started to head out the bedroom doors. With Khepeshef now pharaoh, he asked if she would stay and be his trusted adviser and if Ankh would be the head of his army. Ankh agreed gratefully and headed back to his bedchamber.

He thanked Kepra for her help and asked if she would explain everything to their mom; she agreed.

She sat their mother down and told her, "I know you have questions, and now it is better than any to ask.".

She looked straight at Kepra and said, "I know you, and you refused to tell me who you were when we first spoke. Why?".

Kepra could feel the pain her mother felt from lying to her, but she explained, "I had to be sure before I came to anyone; I wanted to make sure I did my research before I lifted this burden. I'm sorry I didn't tell you sooner, but that little girl you gave away so long ago was me. I have returned to find you firstly, but while I have been here, I see that I also had a connection to this planet, not only because of you but because my people needed me. You... You gave me away, though. So, I don't understand why me not telling you mattered at all.".

Nefertari stood up and rushed to Kepra and hugged her, reassuring her that was not the case at all. "I had to save my people, Kepra; they relied on us to protect them. You think I wanted to give you away?" She cupped her mouth to stop her mouth from whimpering. "I didn't want to give you up, and I did all this for my people. I wanted a better life for them, and you of all people should see that by killing your brother.".

Khepeshef looked at his mother and said, "mother, that is my fault and my fault alone. There is something I did not tell you the day I gave my crown away.".

She looked puzzled. "My brother threatened to kill you and father in your sleep if I was not compliant to step down and hand him the crown.".

She shook her head in disbelief. The former queen said, "no, no, I don't believe you.".

He looked at her for a while and said, "you think I would lie on something so vile? Ask Ankh; he heard everything from just outside the door. What else would have made me just hand over the crown? I have been groomed my whole life for that position; I wanted nothing more but to help our people and for our lands to be prosperous." Khepeshef had tears running down his face. "So, I understand if you are mad, mother, but something had to be done.".

She sat there for a second and then glanced at her two children from Khepeshef to Kepra. Nefertari said, "well, then, isn't it a fitting end to someone who threatened to kill their loved ones in their sleep, that they would die the same way?" They all smiled at each other and hugged each other. Everyone was glad that the tyrant had been finally stopped.

The next day Ankh came in on the family rejoicing from the night before and said, "hey, guys, I'm glad we're all loving this family reunion and all, but it's time to share with Egypt what happened and who their new leader is. A war is coming, and we need the people to be aware.".

Khepeshef opened the doors from the palace to see all his loyal subjects. Word had gotten around of the tyrants demise and they wanted to see the good news for themselves. Khepeshef greeted them with a wave and reassured them the city was finally in good hands. After appeasing the crowd, he went in to continue talking with his family. The former queen looked at Khepeshef and said, "you will have to have a coronation. Show the people we are not worried about anything, that we have everything under control." Everyone settled on the idea and then made plans to hold a feast to welcome the new pharaoh. While preparing for the festivities, it gave Ankh and Kepra time to prepare for the battle. One monster was down, but there was still one left out there.

Kepra had called on the gods to help her with the war that was coming their way. Neith and Horus, along with Thoth, had been given specific military plans from Kepra on how they would attack the witch Heka. Everyone agreed that Heka needed to be stopped for all of humanity and for the gods. Heka was taking over Egypt fast, and she had her mind set on killing anyone who got in her way. At this point, humans bowed and sacrificed everything and anyone they could get their hands on to be in the good graces of the witch Heka. She was a beautiful creature with the mark of the moon on her forehead and her eyes like pools from the dark abyss. They were hypnotizing, and she mesmerized humans with just one glance. She was approaching Thebes, but before she hit the beautiful city to conquer the region, she stopped at Memphis. She wanted to take out Egypt's second most important city before reaching Kepra.

Heka and her army went through the city like a disease; her dark aura was a plague. The buildings fell, the cattle and crops died, and people were in a frenzy. She left one person and horse to inform Kepra she was coming. Heka pulled the frail human by the seams of his garment and said, "lowly human, today is your lucky day. I will let you live on one condition.".

The man said, "anything, anything.".

Heka smiled and pointed toward Thebes. Heka said, "go to Thebes and tell Kepra her city is the only one in Egypt that has not been devoured, but I'm on my way to finish it and her.".

He asked, "the warrior of Egypt?".

Heka hissed in anger and said, "yes!".

The guy, scared and shaking, agreed to the witch's wishes and told her he would.

Chapter 13
A Black Celebration

Thebes was in an uproar not because of the war but because of the coronation of the new pharaoh and the old one gone. The coronation had shifted the villagers 'attention from a negative to a positive. The coronation was prepared to happen at the palace; Kepra was getting her brother ready and was excited for something good to have finally occurred. The ceremony was laced in gold and white with hints of a yellow to honor the sun god. Everyone who was anyone was there. It was an event that would not soon be forgotten. The wealthiest families took part in the ceremony, while the villagers were outside celebrating the new pharaoh in spirit. The event was held in a place that was open in the palace; that way, even though some people couldn't attend, they could at least view it. The pharaoh wanted everyone to feel involved.

As the ceremony was beginning, Ankh asked Kepra if he could talk to her; she straightened her brother's crown and followed Ankh into the hallway. Ankh told her there was a man outside the city gates who wanted to talk to her. She questioned the reason why he would want to talk to her. Ankh said, "he asked for you specifically he wouldn't talk to anyone that wasn't you, it sounded urgent." She agreed and asked him to come with her.

Kepra called on Aten, and she and Ankh rode off to the front of the city. Passing so many of the people in the street, she noticed that everyone was drunk, happy, finally feeling like they could make a living in the city again, not only that but the temples too. They rested easy, knowing their offerings and souls would be safe once again. As Kepra and Ankh approached the city's gates, she noticed a dark fog coming over the desert. The guards opened the gates; there was a man on a horse. Kepra got off the lion, and he got off the horse. She said, "what do you want to from me, traveler?".

He seemed worried and tired, like he had been running from sunup to sundown. He said, "I bring grave news. The wicked one, Heka, is on the way, and she is coming for you. She said to tell you that she had devoured all of Egypt. This is her final stop.".

Kepra, shocked, knew that this would happen. She just didn't expect it to be so soon. Ankh got off the lion and ran to Kepra. He said, "it's ok, Kepra. We have been preparing for this day, remember? We have been training for over five months.".

The guy looked at them both and put his hand on his head, and said, "if she did what she did to Memphis, nothing could prepare you for it. She sneaks into the city unseen, and then after you think she has done all she can, she allows her army of the undead to feast on your flesh and turn you. It was terrifying. She wiped out the entire city within hours; it was like nothing I've ever seen.".

As he talked, she heard screaming coming from behind her. He glanced at the city and said, "she has arrived. I will be leaving. I can't bear to see what she did twice, and whatever she's done, it isn't going to be isn't half as bad as what she wants to do to you. She wants you. Whatever you have done to the witch, say your prayers to the gods because these are your last hours, warrior.".

She thought, gods. I must pray to the gods for help. Kepra, at that moment seeing the buildings fall over the city, hopped on Aten with Ankh; Ankh was worried. He asked her what their plan was. She said to Ankh, "I don't know just yet; I have to rely on the gods. I need their strength and power. That seems like the only thing that's going to give us an advantage here.".

Kepra was stressed about her brother and her parents. She told Aten to hurry up as they flew through falling buildings. As they were riding back to the palace, some creatures were popping up, creatures that skin was dark gray and had eyes like black holes. Kepra thought, there is no way that they got here that quickly.

Heka had devised a plan that was unlike how she took over the other cities. She had been confident that the man she spared to tell Kepra of her coming was also going to give up how she conquered Memphis. Heka knew Kepra would try and prepare for the attack; if given details, she would not let that happen. Heka thought quickly and chose to go through with a sporadic attack, but what Heka didn't know is that the anger she had led her to be vulnerable and gave room for misguided tactics. Heka's attack also left her open to develop a plan thought out by Kepra and her crew.

Kepra, almost to the palace, prayed to Horus, Neith, and Thoth. She even called out to Amun. Amun did not answer, but the other three did. They joined her and rode down from the heavens on a huge falcon, a griffin, and a horse that had fire for wings. The animals were plated with armor from head to toe. Kepra asked the gods to attack all of the undead that were attacking the humans. She told them to be careful, and if they could turn any of the undead back to normal, to please do so. She asked for them to gather all the unaffected people and find shelter and protect them. Once Heka was beaten, they should all return to normal. They agreed and dispersed.

When Kepra returned to the palace, she looked everywhere for her parents and brother, but there was no sign of them anywhere. She looked over where the ceremony was being held and saw her mother in the distance. Her body was on a pillar; she was bloody and dying with gaping wounds. Kepra ran to her with tears in her eyes. She couldn't believe she wasn't more prepared for this; she should have seen this coming. She thought, I could have saved her; I could have saved all of them. She wasn't a warrior of Egypt; how could she be if she let all of Egypt down? Kepra approached her mother; the closer she got, she could see why she was on the pillar in the first place.

Her father was underneath the pillar; she cried as she picked her mother's almost lifeless body in her arms. Her mother coughed up blood and said, "don't be sad, my child. It is just my time; it was written." Kepra then remembered what Anubis had said to her about the two humans. It made sense; her mother, Neith, asked about her mother and father and how much time they had to live. Kepra couldn't think of the reason why she would want to know at that moment. Her mother reached for Kepra's face and said, "my child, I am so glad I got to see the beautiful woman that you grew up to be. I am so grateful to the gods for that.".

Kepra shook her head and said, "why, if I wouldn't have come, you would still be alive. I am nothing; I failed you and father.".

Nefertari said, "my child, there is something I need to tell you before I die because I am afraid you will never know this unless I tell you. Your father.... He is ... he is the king of gods, my love; Amun is your father, and please tell Ankh... Ankh is Ramesses's son.".

As Nefertari said that to her, Kepra shook her head and asked, "what?" But it was too late. Nefertari had passed with Kepra knowing nothing of what her mother was talking about. Kepra walked over to Ankh and Aten and looked around to try to find her brother. Kepra decided to tell Ankh later of what happened with her mother. There was so much going on that Kepra couldn't even begin to comprehend.

Out of nowhere, they heard a scream, which Kepra noticed was from her brother. Kepra darted off in the direction of the scream and found her brother with three guards trying to fight the undead army off. Aten and Ankh, who were right behind Kepra, stood their ground. The undead surrounded the guards and king; Kepra looked at Aten and told him to roar and breathe the breath of the gods. Aten took a long-winded breath, and before he could take the creatures out, Kepra yelled out, "duck!" To her brother and the guards.

The lion set fire to over twelve of the creatures, leaving them singed and unable to get up. Kepra ran to her brother to ask if he was all right; he complied and nodded. "Thank you for coming for me.".

Kepra said, "of course. I will never leave you again." She made sure Khepeshef was all right and then said, "brother, look. I know this isn't the best time to ask but, do you know anything about your father having another child?".

Khepeshef looked and said, "you mean our father?".

She forgot and said, "yes, our father.".

He said, "I'm sure he had many children. Why?".

Kepra looked off and said, "never mind; forget about it. Let's just get you out of here and try to regroup.".

He said ok and followed the three out of the palace along with the soldiers who were left.

Watching the rear end. They were walking to find the gods that had saved the rest of the villagers when all of a sudden, Kepra started hearing whispers. "Kepra, I see you. I'm coming to get you.".

Kepra stopped in her tracks and looked around to see where the witch was. Kepra couldn't find the witch and started getting paranoid; Kepra started talking to her brother about what was happening. She started to feel like she was going insane. "Khepeshef, I hear something. Don't you?".

"Kepra, what are you talking about? I don't hear anything." While she was talking to her brother, a light-gray shadow crept up behind him and went through his body. He started convulsing and dropped to the ground he died immediately. Heka appeared in front of her with.

Heart in hand from her brother. Kepra was so furious, angrier than she had ever been. She started attacking the witch; it was a battle that would rival all.

In Aaru, Amun had heard his daughter's cry; he was devastated he could not help her. He was busy trying to get one of the oldest goddesses contained not to interrupt the fight of Kepra and Heka. He knew he was needed in Aaru.

Kepra was fighting the witch's magic with her sword. With every powerful throw of magic Heka threw at Kepra, Kepra repelled it. Every time Kepra got closer to Heka, the witch would just vanish. There was no touching her. Heka, too, was having a hard time trying to land an attack, and it was a stalemate. Kepra wouldn't take that; she was determined to find a way to kill the witch who hurt her entire family. Kepra thought to herself, I am this monster. I created this thing.

Amun, who finally got Isis to the point where she couldn't go anywhere, went to earth. Amun shot to earth like a shooting star. When he got there, he stopped time; he was in front of Kepra and allowed her movement. Kepra was captivated at the way everything just seemed to stop. Amun appeared in front of her. "Kepra, child, I am your father. I realize you're already aware of that. What you choose to do with those emotions, I cannot stop. It was my decision for your mothers not to inform you. You have searched so long for who your true parents were, when all along, I have been in front of you, watching you, making sure you had every advantage to be the goddess you truly were meant to be. Kepra, you were always a goddess, and I'm sorry that I let you doubt that. I loved your mother as much as I love you, and I want you to know you would win this battle. Use your mind and not your sight to attack something that doesn't want to be seen. You will find the strength, Kepra; it is within you. You are still the most powerful warrior in the world." He then left as quickly as he appeared, and no one had known any different; time went back to normal.

With the uplifting speech her father gave her, she felt ready for war. It was like a light went off in Kepra, and she felt a burning feeling in her soul like she found this unknown power that she never knew she had as a human. She closed her eyes and heard her mother and Horus fighting the undead. There were so many people that Heka turned. It was unreal. Kepra also heard Thoth, her other love, fighting with his magic alongside Horus. Ankh was with Aten to her left, battling as well. She knew that she had to defeat this woman for her and them as well. If she lost, who would protect these people that she loved? So, when she closed her eyes, she remembered her training. It allowed her a certain superhuman strength that played along with her ability to combat. She heard the witch's every step, and as she heard them, she calculated where she would step next. She took out her fangs and released them; she slung her sword to the right where the witch was, not to kill her but to wound her. As the witch screamed, she disappeared to another place right where the fangs were coming in. The witch ducked, and the fangs ricocheted off a nearby pillar. Without the witch's knowledge, the fangs turned around and cut her so deeply that she could not use her magic to escape.

With the poison that set in from the fangs, Heka had no choice but to drop where she was. When she dropped, Kepra went to the witch, brave and determined to reunite with herself completely. Kepra took the witch's head in her lap, looked into her eyes, and said, "we have a short time before you take that last breath, but I wanted you to know that Isis planned this whole thing. You have to be smart enough to see that she used you to get to me. She played you, Heka.

The whole time you thought you were in control, you weren't. She let you think that. She played me too. She knew I was human and that with me being such, I could never defeat a god, but I did. We can show her that we prevailed, Heka. We can be in control once more.".

Heka, barely alive, agreed and whispered, "so where do we go from here?".

Kepra said, "join me in my body once again, and let's take this battle to Aaru and win the war, instead of the battle. Let us unite and promise to stop her. If evil steps in our path ever again, let us always be in control of our destiny." Heka reached for Kepra's face, and gold-and white light shot from her body into Kepra. They were finally one again. Kepra was now the warrior witch. All the power that Heka gained was now Kepra's as well. Kepra was unstoppable. Kepra's eyes became gold, and her body radiated a gold aura around it.

It was time to take the fight that Isis wanted so badly to her. Horus and the other gods who were on earth saw the power radiating from Kepra. They had never seen anything like it. Before Kepra left for Aaru, she looked around at her city, and the people were changing back. Earth had been saved, but it would need much more work repairing all the damage Heka had done.

Chapter 14

Demigod

Kepra, knowing that the earth was safe, decided to go back to Aaru to finish what was started. She placed one knee on the ground and then shot up to the heavens. When Kepra got to the gate of Aaru, she could see the once ethereal place was now gloomy and filled with colors of blood red and hints of orange. Horus had got there just before Kepra could proceed into the palace. "Kepra!" He yelled. "Before you do this, please remember that she is still my mother; as crazy and demented as she may seem, I still love her. If you can help it, do not kill her. Banish her; do anything else. I cannot bear to witness my mother's death. Consider it, I beg you; you just saw your mother die in your arms. Don't make me go through what you just had to see.".

She looked at him and saw sadness in his eyes. She remembered, even with the pulsing witch blood running through her veins. Kepra looked at him and uttered, "I will try, Horus, but I promise you nothing.".

When she arrived, Amun-ra was fighting with Isis. Kepra began to get more furious. Amun was the only real parent she had left; she was not about to let Isis take him from her. Kepra let out a loud warrior cry. She jolted in between the two and took out her sword, flipping it back and forth in her hands. Her sword began to show a glow like never before. Kepra remembered soon after her father saying to her that she would tap into the power of the sword when the time was right. She looked at the sword and swung it around slowly to get the feel of it. It was producing so much power that she could barely contain herself or the sword. Kepra got ahold of herself; she focused all this immense power into her mind. Instead of the power using her, she had to use it. Suddenly, Isis yelled out to Kepra, "little warrior, you think you can kill me? Ha ha ha ha." She laughed hard. "I am more powerful than you or your father. Oh, yes, I finally found out who you were; I'm assuming you did too.".

Kepra looked at her, confused. "You knew, didn't you? All along that he was my father. Yet you still said nothing when I came to you." She was furious.

"Silly girl," Isis said. "I owe you nothing; your father thought you were some special prophecy that would save all the gods and all of Egypt. I will enjoy seeing all the gods fear me when I have eradicated you and your father. Then I will rule the gods and the rest of the world." She laughed maniacally. Kepra couldn't bear it anymore. She took off irrationally and swung the sword toward the evil witch. Isis said one word, and a magic illusion appeared. It made a gray smoke, and all of a sudden, six Isis were running around. She knew that it wasn't real, but she had to determine which one was the real Isis. Kepra had to rely on her training yet again. So, she closed her eyes one more time and listened for the witch. She heard the witch's breathing coming from the one in the middle of the six. She took a second and ran toward it, nicking a piece of the goddess. Isis cried in pain and began to make more magic appear. She hit her with a flame of fire, and Kepra hit it with her sword, making the ball of fire ricochet off the metal and hitting the witch.

Isis, badly in pain, tried to freeze the warrior; Kepra stopped midair in a jump and was frozen from within her body. She couldn't move; it was as if time itself froze again. Isis slung the warrior on the ground with her hair, breaking the freeze spell she had put on her. Kepra fell to the ground, falling so hard it made it almost impossible for her to get back up, but she staggered to get up. Blood dripping from her, she placed one leg on the floor and leaned on the sword's blade to help her up.

Kepra stopped and closed her eyes. She heard a voice from within her telling her, "I am with you, Kepra. Let me help you." Kepra's body started to generate a lot of mana; all Kepra's wounds seemed to have healed. Isis could feel Kepra's energy spike; Isis turned around, only to see the warrior standing up, ready for round two.

Kepra ran to the witch with a full-force sword in hand and struck the god. No amount of magic could protect her this time. When Kepra hit the witch, she stumbled and fell, begging for her life. Kepra approached with eyes no longer gold but white. Every part of the warrior was gleaming with golden rays. Kepra thought for a quick second of what Horus said to her before she entered the palace; Kepra looked at her and said, "Horus blesses you, and for his sake, I will not take your life, witch. I will let my father determine what he wants to do with you.".

Kepra turned around and began to walk away; after Kepra turned her back, Isis tried to fire another spell. Horus saw what was about to happen. Immediately, he stepped in and before he had a chance to throw a landing hit, the witch disappeared. Horus looked around in confusion. Amun looked at Kepra and Horus and told them that he wasn't going to let either one kill Isis. He didn't want to have Horus go through life having killed his mother, nor did he want Kepra having a rift with Horus for doing it. So Amun said, "I decided to banish her to the unknown. She will eventually return, but by then, I will have something to do with her.".

The heavens had become white again, and everyone was rejoicing. Kepra had defeated the witch in Egypt and the heavens, and the heavens were about to celebrate. Before she could celebrate with her fellow gods, she had to see Egypt and help Ankh and them repair the beautiful country. As the gods prepared for the celebration of a lifetime, Kepra walked over to Amun. She looked at him for a couple of seconds. "don't you want to say something to me, old man?".

He looked at her confused and said, "what? Thank you for helping the gods?".

"Nooo," she said. "don't you want to apologize? You kept a huge secret from me that you could have told me way before now.".

He said, "no, Kepra, I don't want to apologize because everything I did was to prepare you for today, to help you be the woman who is in front of me.".

She looked at him with tears in her eyes. "You did nothing for me; I did everything for myself. You're my father; you could've helped me. There was not so much as a sign that you were there for me.".

Amun looked at Kepra and said, "I have never left you; I have always been there for you since the day you were born. I remember the first day that I saw your mother, beautiful on the balcony of the palace in Egypt while the sun was just setting. Tears were running down her face. She had just found out that Ramesses had a child on the way with one of their servants and shortly after he left for another battle leaving her without the explanation she deserved. I heard her prayers for her husband and quickly directed my full attention to her. I made myself human within those few months Ramesses was gone. Before I left, I laid with her, and you were born on the full moon in December. I have always made sure you were ok. The day you touched the earth when you left Aaru, I was the one who made sure you had your weapons. Do you remember where you got your armor from? The mute man? That was me. I've always made sure you were taken care of, Kepra, because you have always been my responsibility.

I'm sorry we did not tell you sooner but the night I left your mother and told her who I really was, I begged her to keep it a secret from you and Ramesses. I had to insure you had a normal life, but the fates had different plans for you than I did. I'm so happy you have finally become one with yourself and found out who you are, my child.".

Kepra looked at her father and wept. She ran into his arms and thanked him for everything he'd done for her. She had no idea he was looking out for her like he was. She took a step back from hugging him and looked at him with tears still in her eyes. She said, "father, I have a request; I would like to stay on the planet to help the people there. I think there are a lot of cities that still need help. Being in action and being able to change history physically can be my blessing to these people and my job as your daughter.".

He nodded and understood; he told her if she needed anything to pray, and he would answer. Neith looked at the warrior talking to Amun and began to approach her daughter. Neith said, "Kepra, I know that me being your mother was a lie that I told you on behalf of your father, but I loved you nonetheless.".

Kepra, with tears still streaming down her face, hugged her mom and told her, "And you are still my mother. You will always be thank you for making me who I am without creating me." When Neith and Kepra stopped hugging, she looked at her, nodded her head, and walked over to her pet and hopped on Aten to return to earth.

Horus and Thoth ran over to her before she left and said, "Kepra, what about us?".

Kepra pulled Horus to the side. Thoth in the background said, "sure, falcon boy, why not?".

Kepra hugged Horus and said, "Horus, I love you, and I will pray to you often to give me strength in my battles. Hopefully, you will find the time to visit me.".

"I will never leave you. I love you as well, and I will always hope for our future together" Horus said.

She kissed him and then went over to Thoth. "Thoth, you are my mentor, but more importantly, a friend. I will never forget you.".

Thoth hugged her and said, "so you have chosen?" Kepra scratched her head. "What are you talking about?".

"Do you remember back in the library, I said one day you would have to choose? Well, I can see that you have.".

"Thoth, it's not like that. I am not going to be with anyone; I'm going to Egypt to help my people, your people, Thoth.".

"So, you will be the god among men?" He said.

"Something like that, yes," she said as she began to pet Aten. Kepra hopped on Aten's back one again to leave, she waved goodbye to everyone, and took off on Aten. As she was leaving, all the gods were by the gate waving goodbye back to her.

Amun yelled out to her and said, "you are always welcome here, my child." Kepra blew a kiss and then flew off into the cosmos.

Earth was only a short distance ahead of them. Kepra was excited to see everyone again. She knew she still owed Ankh an explanation. Aten and Kepra stopped in Pi-Ramesses first to see Ankh. When Kepra touched down, she saw the city still in shambles. She looked around, and the people who had been converted to the undead by Heka were all normal now. The citizens from different cities were still in disarray, and they were trying to understand how and why they were in Pi-Ramesses. Among all the chaos, she saw Ankh helping his people; she quickly ran to see him. As she approached, the guards were already looking to him to help them. They needed guidance; they took the former pharaohs and prince to the palace for a proper burial. He sensed someone approaching him. He turned to look, and it was Kepra. They ran to each other, and he was so happy to see her. She looked around and said, "you've done well getting these people the help they need.".

He said, "yeah, I couldn't have done it without your help; you saved the people of Egypt, Kepra. What brings you back here? I thought you would be in Aaru celebrating.".

"Uh, yeah, well, I wanted to be here on earth. I wanted to help you and our people repair Egypt," she said. "Ankh, I must ask you something, though. How did your parents die again? I know its random, but I have to know.".

He said, "I never met my father; I just heard he was in the military for the pharaoh. My mother worked in the palace as well, and she was the queen's handmaiden.".

Kepra asked if his mother ever talked about his father to him. He said, "no, only what I have told you.".

She told him, "Ankh, I think I know why you haven't ever heard that much about your father.".

He looked at her confused. "What do you mean, Kepra?".

"Before my mother died, she told me who my father was, and also who your father was. Ankh, your father, never worked for the pharaoh. Your father was the pharaoh; you're the next king in line. I can't believe I didn't see it; the reddish tint on your hair is only from a Ramesses descendent.".

He asked Kepra, "so did you get the real reason your mother gave you to the gods?".

She replied, "that I did not get an answer to. Still, the only logical explanation is that my father had bigger and better things for my destiny rather than portraying life as the princess of Egypt." Kepra looked at Ankh and said, "it is time to tell your people. They deserve to know the truth. They deserve a new start, and so do you.".

Chapter 15
Protector of All

It took years for Egypt to get back to how it was before, but with love and dedication, it eventually did. Egypt had an amazing warrior pharaoh leading them that did whatever it took in his power to make sure he stayed in the gods 'good graces. Ankh had been getting his infantry and palace in order. Kepra had been traveling around Egypt to see if anyone was in need and if she could help. It was that time of the year again when the opet festival was getting near, and everyone gathered to celebrate the great god Amun. It was a festival that lasted for days on end. Kepra decided to see how the new king was holding up with his position. She sneaked into the palace undetected. She slowly approached the king's quarters, where he was sitting on his bed. She said, "long day, great pharaoh?".

He looked up with uncertainty and saw the warrior goddess. His eyes lit up, and he was so excited to see her. He said, "no, I was actually just thinking about you, and ironically you show up. Are you sure you're not a full god?" He asked.

She chuckled and denied his claim. "It is my father's celebration. I decided to see the festivities and you.".

He looked at her and then got up and started to head over by her. He grabbed her, and they hugged while giggling. "Kepra, my offer still stands. I will never marry another because my heart belongs to you. I want you to be my wife.".

She looked at him and backed away from his arms. "Ankh, you know I love you, but I can't be with anyone. I have a greater duty than to be a queen. I have no desire for the people to know me as their pharaoh but as their hero. I will be the voice for the people when there is none. I don't mind coming by and seeing you from time to time because I miss you, but being your wife is not something I can be. I hope you understand, Ankh.".

He looked at her with tears in his eyes and said, "like I said, I will never marry another, Kepra." He looked out the window with the sounds of the guards approaching, and when he looked back at her, she was gone. All that was left was the smell of her.

Kepra ended up traveling along the red sea with Aten. She loved the lush greenery and water. She was still having love affairs with Thoth and Horus, but she never forgot about Ankh. She never saw him in person again due to the fact she knew he needed to move on. He had a duty to carry out the lineage of the great Ramesses. Word had eventually got to her about a wedding for the new pharaoh, and she was truly happy for him. She and Aten were the protectors of Egypt; no one would be in need under her protection again and not receive it.